TWISTED LIVES

SUSAN K. DRONEY

This is a work of fiction. Names, characters, places, and incidents are products of the author's imagination or are used fictitiously and are not to be construed as real. Any resemblance to actual events, locations, organizations, or persons, living or dead, is entirely coincidental.

World Castle Publishing, LLC

Pensacola, Florida
Copyright © Susan K. Droney 2017
Paperback ISBN: 9798891263925
eBook ISBN: 9781629898292
Second Edition World Castle Publishing, LLC, November 27, 2017
http://www.worldcastlepublishing.com

Licensing Notes

Cover: Karen Fuller
Editor: Maxine Bringenberg

Table of Contents

Chapter One

Lightning streaked through the late afternoon sky, followed by ear splitting cracks of thunder. Rain pelted the lifeless form lying on the sodden ground.

"Trevors, get over here!"

Daniel Trevors moved away from the crowd of curious onlookers that had gathered, at the same time wondering what it was about tragedies that brought people out. He motioned to two officers to relieve him, and then rushed to his partner Ben Wilson's side.

"Look at this." Ben pointed at the corpse lying face down.

Daniel squinted, and then focused to where Ben was pointing. He examined the puncture wounds in the man's jacket. "He must have been stabbed twenty times!" He looked at his partner. "You don't think this is connected with the other three, do you, Ben?"

Wilson shrugged. "What do you think?"

"I think we have a serial killer on our hands."

****

Zoey Davis stared at the cloudburst from the window of her dance studio. Lightning streaked through the darkened sky. She hoped the storm would let up before her class ended, and at the same time wondered if her students for the next class would show up. She didn't want to reschedule if she could help it, because it would mean giving up a day she had planned for something else.

She felt a tug at her arm and turned away from the window. "What is it, Jessi?" she asked with a smile, looking into the child's frightened eyes.

"I'm afraid of the storm," Jessi answered in a quivering voice. "The lightning scares me."

"It'll soon be over," she said soothingly. "Go back to the bar and work on your stretching exercises with the other girls. I'll be there in a minute." She patted the child's shoulder, and then watched as the six year old cautiously made her way over to the bar.

Zoey turned back to the window, staring again at the raging storm. Her mood suddenly became as black as the sky. Her life was a mess, and she had no one to blame but herself. Her life could have been perfect, but she'd selfishly thrown it all away. Her eyes narrowed. She had to make some hard decisions about her life. No matter what she did, there would be harsh consequences.

****

Daniel Trevors opened the door to the Davis Dance Studio. He walked inside the lobby and removed his raincoat. He heard music coming from a closed door and quietly opened it and peeked inside. He smiled at the group of young dancers as they twisted and turned their bodies in an attempt to imitate their teacher.

Zoey caught his eye and nodded at him. "Okay, young ladies, that's it for today. I'll see you on Thursday." She picked up a towel and mopped her forehead as she made her way over to where he stood.

"Hi, Daniel. Has the rain stopped?"

"Almost. That was quite a storm."

"It was." Her eyebrows knitted together. "What brings you here, Daniel?"

"I was in the neighborhood, so I thought I'd drop in for a minute to say hello." His eyes swept around the studio. "You've done a great job with this place. I still can't believe the transformation."

"Thank you. At times I wondered if I'd made the biggest mistake of my life. We're only a half hour from Philadelphia, and I was afraid potential students would rather go there than take a chance on me."

"No. I think they wanted something closer to home. After all, Vickville isn't exactly a little rinky dink town."

"I know. It's just that it made me wonder why the former studios couldn't make a go of it here."

"They didn't have your drive. It was just a hobby to them. Look at you today."

"It was really a mess, wasn't it?" she said with a laugh, tossing her pretty blonde head.

"Yeah, it was." He grinned. He remembered only too well how deplorable this property had been when she'd excitedly showed it to him, seeing the possibilities that he hadn't been able to see. Even though he'd thought it was a vast waste of her time and money, he had admired Zoey's vision of what it could be with a little hard work. Her energy and enthusiasm had known no bounds, and her endless hours spent scrubbing, painting, and refinishing every inch of her studio resulted in a bright and cheerful room, which she had proudly opened to the public less than a year later. It wasn't long until the studio was filled to capacity with students. "I still can't believe that this is the same property."

She smiled. "As I recall, you weren't very supportive in the beginning."

"I tried to be, but I was afraid it wouldn't work out and I didn't want to see your dreams go up in smoke."

"Neither did I," she admitted, "since I put every dime I had into the place." She threw her towel on a chair. "I've got a few minutes until my next class. Can I get you anything?"

"No, thanks," he answered.

She looked curiously at him. "Daniel, your eyes always give you away. When they're dark and brooding like they are now, I know something's wrong. Quit trying to hide behind a smile." She frowned. "What is it, Daniel? I know this isn't a social call. Is Taylor okay?"

"Taylor's fine." He looked at Zoey for a long minute. "I don't want to alarm you, Zoey, but there's been another murder...a few doors down from here."

She stared wide-eyed at him. "That's four in the past month! What's going on?" she asked, her voice becoming high-pitched.

He drew her into his arms, hoping to calm her trembling body. "Please be careful, Zoey," he said softly, gently running a hand over her shoulder. He felt her stiffen. "What's wrong?" he whispered.

She pulled away from him. "I told you how I feel."

His eyes narrowed. "You did. You made it perfectly clear."

"Daniel, we'll never be more than friends. What we had before is over. Please don't expect anything else." She picked up her ballet shoes. "I've got to get ready for my next class."

"I wasn't expecting anything."

"Thanks for stopping by."

Daniel watched her closely as she changed her shoes. His

eyes traveled over the length of her body. Her leotard clung to her shapely and fit figure. Her energy amazed him; it always had. He often wondered how she built the stamina to sustain the rigid demands her many classes put on her. She was one hell of a woman. There was no doubt about that. And he wanted her back.

He walked to the door, opened it, turned, and looked at her again. She had such a powerful hold on him that no matter how many months passed, he couldn't rid his mind of her. She consumed his thoughts day and night. He wanted her to love him the way she used to. He would never understand why she'd abruptly ended it with him. He hadn't seen it coming and was completely blindsided. They'd been happy, in love and making plans. He'd spent many lonely nights racking his brain trying to come up with a possible reason for their break up, but there was none. He'd picked himself up and thrown himself into his work, but still he couldn't get her out of his system.

She waved to him. He smiled, waved goodbye, and then slowly left the studio.

He had a long night ahead of him, and he wasn't looking forward to it. A cold-blooded killer lurked somewhere in the shadows, and his instincts told him that it was only a matter of time before the murderer would strike again.

****

Zoey walked the six blocks to her apartment enjoying the freshness of the evening after the earlier heavy rain. Bright stars lit the sky, and a light breeze made it a perfect night for a walk. She wished her mind was as clear as the night, but Daniel invaded her thoughts. He wanted something from her that she was incapable of giving to him or any other man. If things were different, she knew he would have her heart. In a way he still did. She loved everything about him…his warm smile, the laugh lines around his beautiful dark eyes, his slim, but firm build. But most of all, she loved his genuine compassion for others. She admired him for the way he raised his daughter, and still gave his all to his work. He seemed to have an endless reserve of energy. When he said he was available day or night, he really meant it.

Zoey reached her apartment building, slipped inside, and slammed the heavy security door shut. She pulled the mail from her box, and then by-passed the elevator and walked the three flights to her apartment. Once inside, she slipped off her shoes and carried them to her bedroom. She was tired, but knew that going to bed now would only mean hours of tossing and turning, so she grabbed a book from the nightstand table, walked to the bathroom, and drew a bubble bath.

****

Daniel sat at his cluttered desk with his eyes focused on a stack of files, all needing his attention. He rubbed his jaw. The murders plaguing Vickville made the other cases seem trivial by comparison. Four murders with no clues or possible motives. The killer was slick, but somewhere, somehow, he'd slip up. Someone knew something. He gulped his coffee and signed a few reports.

"Ready to call it a night?" Ben called to him from his desk.

Daniel closed a folder and stood. "Yeah, the rest of these can wait until tomorrow. Lately I've been spending more time here than at home. When I am home I'm only there long enough to grab a few hours of sleep, and I'm back here again." He stretched.

Ben grinned. "So what else is new? But all work and no play makes Ben a dull boy. I think I'll go to Vito's for a couple. Care to join me?" he asked, pulling on his jacket.

Daniel glanced at his wristwatch. "Not tonight, Ben. Thanks anyway."

"Got a hot date?" Ben teased.

"Don't I wish? Nah, I've got to get home. I need to touch base with Taylor."

"Such are the demands of single parenthood. But you're lucky. Taylor's a good kid. She's not running the streets like half the teens around here."

He nodded. "I'm very fortunate. I just wish I could figure out a way to spend more time with her. I was thinking about taking her to New York for a weekend next month. She loves musicals."

"Sounds like a plan. That's if we ever get a weekend off again." Ben cocked an eye. "I'd love to drive to the city myself. It's been a while. Only a couple of hours away, but it feels like it's across the country."

"I know." Daniel scratched his chin. "So close and yet so far away."

Ben slapped him on the back. "Well, I'm going to run, then. See you tomorrow."

Daniel watched Ben as he exited the office. Ben was a couple of years older than Daniel, but acted like he was ten years younger. He was good looking and had an animal magnetism that drew women to him. He'd recently been through a bitter divorce following ten years of a stormy marriage, which Daniel knew was in part because of Ben's infidelity. He partied every night with a different woman, and loved telling Daniel of his escapades. On more than one occasion he'd tried to set Daniel up, but each time Daniel had firmly refused.

Ben was a good cop and his instincts were sharp, but Daniel saw the loneliness etched on Ben's face every year as the holidays drew near. Ben's ex, Clare, had moved across the country, making it impossible for Ben to have much of a relationship with his only child, Josh. Josh was the only good thing the marriage had produced, and Daniel knew that Ben would do anything for his son. Daniel had, on several occasions, tried to reach out to Ben, but Ben had shrugged him off, telling him he was fine. But Daniel knew differently. On the outside Ben appeared fine, but on the inside he was broken. Daniel knew what that felt like…he'd been there himself.

Daniel set his coffee cup next to the coffee pot and then grabbed his jacket. Half an hour later, he pulled into his garage. After locking the garage, he walked up the front sidewalk of his comfortable home, making a mental list of chores to do around the house when time permitted. He noticed that every light in the house was on. He smiled, as he was certain the electric company did every month when they sent him his bill. Taylor always left every light burning until he was safely home.

"Hi, Dad," his fourteen year old daughter greeted him as he opened the door.

"Hello, honey," he answered, throwing his keys on the entrance hall table. He walked into the living room and sat in his easy chair, then pulled off his shoes, wriggling his toes. "Is your homework finished?" he asked.

"Yeah, I didn't have too much." Taylor sat on the sofa. "I cleaned the house, Dad, and I have your dinner warming in the oven…meat loaf."

He smiled. "Taylor, you don't have to clean and cook all the time. I'll look into hiring a housekeeper. I want you to have some fun."

"I don't mind, Dad. Honest. Besides, we had a housekeeper up until a year ago. Why spend money when I can do the chores myself? Besides, I love cooking. You don't like it?"

"I love your cooking. I just don't want you to spend all of your free time cooking and cleaning. You need to spend more time with your friends and your activities."

"I do, Dad. And don't forget I take dance classes." She stood up. "Do you want me to get your dinner?"

"I'll get it in a few minutes. I just want to unwind first." He stretched his legs.

"I guess I'll go to bed, then. I have a science test tomorrow," she said, making a face.

"You'll do fine as usual, honey," he said confidently.

After she left the room, he picked up the evening paper. After glancing at it for a few minutes, he tossed it aside, then leaned back in his chair and closed his eyes. His mind drifted through the dark recesses of his memories to a place he kept hidden from the world, but which still managed to creep out of the silence to haunt him from time to time. Back then he thought the world was his for the taking. He had everything he wanted and was happy and very contented.

His wife Becky and he had just purchased this house, and were comfortably settling in with their new baby daughter Taylor. He still couldn't remember when Becky had begun to change. It had happened so subtly. After a while, little things that bothered her grew into mountains. When he suggested having another child, she had put him off repeatedly with the same answer: One is enough. Today, looking back, he knew that was the best choice considering what Taylor had endured the first ten years of her life. He would always feel guilty for the abuse his child had suffered at the hands of her own mother. He'd been so wrapped up in his career that he hadn't noticed what was going on under his own roof.

Daniel looked at a framed photo of Taylor. He'd taken the photo last spring, and it now had a prominent spot on the wall. How she resembled Becky. Looking at the photo reminded him of all his child had silently endured. How had he missed all the warning signs? They'd been there, and he'd missed every one. Becky had sunk into a deep depression, and he'd desperately tried to pull her out of it. He'd cut back some of his hours and lavished her with gifts, flowers, candy, nights out on the town, but nothing worked. He couldn't make her happy. He began to think that the problem was him, not Becky. Her depression deepened when he was around, and seemed to lesson when she was alone with their daughter. Becky was a model mother, loving and attentive. Taylor appeared happy and normal. Daniel decided the best thing he could do was to throw himself even deeper into his career, and hope that in time whatever was bothering Becky she would share with him. He wanted his marriage to work, and he would do everything humanly possible to save it. He'd give Becky the space she needed.

He never saw the signs that his bubbly daughter was slowly withdrawing from activities, friends, and even him. She was like a vibrant spring flower that had withered and died once the first sharp bite of autumn had covered it. Most nights she was already tucked into bed when he came home from work. On the days he didn't go in to work early, Taylor had left for school by the time he got up. On his days off, he tried to spend quality time with her, but it wasn't enough to notice that she, too, was withdrawing.

On a bright and sunny day, reality hit him between the eyes when he received an emergency call to come to Taylor's elementary school. He had no inkling that within minutes his life would be drastically changed forever. He was ushered into the principal's office, where Taylor sat huddled in a chair with her head bowed.

He rushed over to her, gathering her into his arms. "Don't you feel well, honey?" he asked softly.

Slowly she lifted her head. Her eyes held no emotion and

appeared to stare through him. But Daniel was more concerned with what he saw. "My God!" he choked. "Who did this to her? What kind of school are you running here? She's only ten years old!" His stomach churned as his facial muscles tightened. His eyes were wide as he stared in disbelief at his daughter's bruised cheek and swollen eye.

"This didn't happen here, Mr. Trevors," the principal, Joe Johnson, answered. "Her teacher sent her to me when Taylor arrived at school this morning." His thin face was rigid.

"Then who did this?" he demanded.

"She refuses to say. Someone from Child Protective Services will be here shortly."

Daniel stiffened. "CPS? Are you accusing me, Mr. Johnson?" He eyed him coldly.

"No one is accusing you, Mr. Trevors. This is standard procedure," Johnson answered. "Since Taylor refuses to tell us what happened, maybe she'll tell you."

"Taylor, who did this to you, baby?" he asked, turning his attention back to his daughter.

Taylor lowered her head. "I'm okay, Daddy."

"Please tell us who did this. Did this happen on the bus?"

"I can't tell, Daddy."

"Did you call my wife?" Daniel asked the principal.

"There was no answer."

Daniel's jaw tightened. Where the hell was Becky? She didn't mention any appointments this morning. Taylor needed her mother.

"Did you try her cell phone?" Daniel looked pointedly at Johnson.

"Yes, several times, but it went to voicemail."

Daniel clenched his fists into tight balls. Why the hell did she have a cell phone if she wasn't going to answer it? Normally he might have been alarmed, but from past experience he knew that Becky had a habit of not answering the phone. Shortly after their marriage, he'd rushed home after trying in vain to reach her, only to be greeted by her sitting serenely on the sofa reading a book. She often times turned off the ringer when she didn't want to be disturbed. No matter how many times he warned her that she shouldn't turn off the ringer, especially when Taylor started school, she blew it off, insisting if the school couldn't reach her then they would contact him.

If it wasn't for the loving maternal way she interacted with Taylor, he might have been concerned. He was determined to have it out with Becky once and for all, and insist that the ringers never again be turned off on the landline or her cell phone. His eyes narrowed. But that would have to wait. Their daughter had been brutally assaulted, and he intended to get to the bottom of it. He forced himself to control the rage boiling to the surface. Someone would pay for harming his child. He looked at Principal Johnson. From his body language, Daniel surmised that Johnson knew more than he was saying.

The door opened and Johnson's secretary escorted a young, attractive woman and two police officers inside the room. Daniel walked over to the officers, both of whom he knew well. "Look at my kid! I want some answers, now!"

"So do we," Officer Brian Milborn replied.

The woman instantly turned her attention to Daniel. "Mr. Trevors, I'm Johanna Mason." She showed him her credentials. "May I question your daughter?"

Daniel glared coldly at her. "What the hell is going on?" he demanded. "Why won't anyone tell me what happened to my daughter?"

16

Officer Dale Cohen laid a hand on Daniel's arm. "We'll get to the bottom of it, Daniel. In this type of case, you know the procedure," he answered sympathetically.

Daniel shook his head, and then threw up his hands. "All right," he said as calmly as he could. "Will someone please tell me what is going on?"

"That's what we intend to find out, Mr. Trevors," Johanna answered. "I need to ask Taylor some questions."

"Ask her what you need to," he said.

She walked over to Taylor. "Hi, Taylor." She seated herself in a chair facing the child.

Taylor shyly raised her eyes. "Hi," she answered in a barely audible voice.

Daniel took several deep breaths and slowly let them out. He felt like he was suffocating in the small office. The woman started her questioning by getting Taylor to talk about her friends, school, and then her home life. He thought the questions would never end, but when they did, he knew that he would never be the same. And neither would his daughter.

"Taylor, will you tell me who did this to you?" Johanna asked gently.

Taylor's eyes grew wide with fear. She bit her trembling bottom lip.

"Was it one of your friends?" the social worker coaxed.

The child shook her blonde head.

"Did it happen at school?" the social worker prodded gently.

She shrugged her shoulders.

Daniel was rapidly losing his patience. "Honey, please tell us what happened," he demanded. "You need to tell us so whoever did this to you can be stopped from hurting you again." His words came out soft and soothing, but inside he knew what he

17

would like to do to the person who had attacked his child.

Taylor looked into her father's eyes.

"Come on, honey. Please tell us."

Her eyes brimmed with tears, then spilled over. "Mommy," she whispered.

"Mommy will be here soon, baby," Daniel said, as he protectively put an arm around her. Her small body stiffened. "What's the matter? What are you afraid of? Mommy and Daddy will protect you." He wished Becky would answer her damned phone. He would have gone home and dragged her here, but there was no way in hell he would leave his child. He nodded to the officers. "Will one of you drive over to my house to see if my wife is there? If she is, bring her down here."

"I'll go," Officer Cohen replied.

Johanna studied Taylor. "Did your mother do this to you?"

"Oh, come on," Daniel said angrily. "Her mother would never—"

"Yes," Taylor choked. "Yes. Mommy hit me." Her body trembled.

Daniel's eyes grew wide. "What?"

"Can you tell us why she did this, Taylor?" Johanna continued.

Taylor nodded.

"Was this the first time your Mommy hit you?"

She shook her head. "I'm bad a lot."

Daniel felt like he'd been punched in the stomach. He couldn't comprehend how this could have been going on right in front of him without a clue. Or were there clues that he had failed to act upon? He'd never seen that side of his wife.

"What happened this morning?" Johanna asked softly.

Taylor sniffed. "I wasn't careful."

"Can you tell me about it, Taylor?"

18

She looked into the woman's eyes. "I spilled my milk."

Daniel's jaw clenched.

"Honey, everybody has accidents." She smiled. "I'm always spilling something."

"But Mommy gets mad." Her voice was low. "Only bad kids make messes."

"Taylor, that's not true," Johanna answered. "Did she punish you every time you spilled something?"

She nodded. "If I tell, then I'll get locked up."

Daniel became nauseous. "What do you mean, baby?" he asked in a cracked voice. "Who's going to lock you up?"

She reached her arms out to her father. "Daddy, don't send me away," she whimpered. "I'm trying to be good. Don't tell Mommy I told you."

Daniel gathered her in his arms and held her close. "Taylor, Daddy would never send you away. Did Mommy tell you that I would?"

"Yes," she said in a barely audible voice.

Daniel looked at Johanna and saw the sympathy in her eyes. "Tell us what Mommy told you. Please?"

Taylor shuddered as she took a deep breath. "Mommy said you wouldn't believe me. If I was bad you would send me to a place where all bad boys and girls go, and you and her would never see me again," she cried. "You would get a new little girl who wouldn't make messes."

"I would never send you away, honey. I love you." His voice cracked as he choked out the words. "I'll never let anyone hurt you again."

"I don't need to ask her any further questions," Johanna said.

Daniel held Taylor for a few minutes until she'd calmed down a little. "What now?" he asked, turning his attention to the social worker.

"We'll wait until your wife gets here."

"Any word on my wife?" Daniel asked Officer Milborn.

"Yes. Officer Cohen found her at home and is driving her here."

Ten minutes later, as Daniel sat with Taylor cradled in his arms, Becky burst into the room, followed by Officer Cohen. She was dressed to perfection, with every hair on her blonde head in place.

All eyes turned to her. If she noticed, she didn't seem to care. Daniel wondered if she was even aware.

Becky rushed over to Daniel and Taylor.

"Don't come near us!" Daniel shouted.

She stopped in her tracks. "What did you say?"

Daniel saw the confusion in her eyes and heard it in her voice, but he didn't care. "You heard me, Becky. Stay away from us."

"I...I don't understand, Daniel." She reached out to touch his arm.

He pushed her hand aside. "I said get away from us."

"I want my daughter!" she cried. "What happened to my baby?"

Taylor lifted her head from her father's shoulder. She stared at her mother. "Don't make me go with her, Daddy," she whispered in Daniel's ear. "She'll be mad that I told."

"Oh, no! Who did this to my baby?" Becky screamed. "Tell me!"

Daniel was stunned. How could she stand there and deny abusing her own child? He stared in disbelief at her.

Becky began ranting, raving, and threatening to sue the school if they didn't tell her who had abused her child.

Could she possibly not know that the abuse Taylor suffered

was from her own hands? If not, she was putting on one hell of a good act. He didn't know what to do. So many emotions flooded through him at once. He despised her for what she had done to their daughter, but at the same time pitied her if she honestly had no comprehension of committing these vile acts against her own child...a child she had nurtured in her womb. His eyes narrowed.

Carrying Taylor safely in his arms, he walked over to the officers, principal, and Johanna Mason. The group stood looking at Becky.

"Taylor, let's go out to lunch," Becky was saying. "Maybe Daddy can get away from work to join us." She looked hopefully at Daniel. "What do you say, honey?"

Taylor grabbed Daniel's hand. "No, Daddy...please! Don't make me go with her."

"It's okay, baby," he whispered. "I won't let her hurt you ever again."

"Taylor, do as I said!" Becky shouted. "You don't want to upset Mommy, now do you?"

"Don't hit me again, Mommy!"

"What did you tell them, Taylor?" Her eyes blazed. "You know what's going to happen now, don't you?"

Daniel's blood ran cold at the shrill voice. This was not the woman he knew. He glanced at Johanna. "She's not in her right mind."

Johanna nodded. "Let me take Taylor to another room."

"Okay." He set his daughter down and she clung to him. "It's okay, honey. Go with Ms. Mason. I'll come get you in a little while."

"Is there an office I can take Taylor to?" Johanna asked the principal.

"Of course," Mr. Johnson replied. "Go through this door."

21

He pointed to a door behind Daniel.

Johanna took Taylor's hand. "It's okay, honey," she whispered as she led Taylor from the room.

"Where are you taking my daughter?" Becky screamed. "Bring her back, you bitch!" She lunged toward Johanna, but the officers stepped in front of her, restraining her arms. "Daniel, do something! Why are you just standing there like an idiot?" She pursed her lips. "I'll have all of you brought up on charges."

Daniel stood looking in disbelief at his wife as she continued spewing her threats laced with language he'd never before heard her utter. He wished he could look deep inside her mind to gain some understanding of what was happening to her.

She suddenly stopped her ranting. Her forehead furrowed and she looked confused.

"Daniel, what's happening?" she asked softly. "Why am I here? What happened to Taylor?" She tried to free herself from the officers, who still held her arms. "Please let go of me." Tears spilled from her eyes. "Daniel, please hold me. I'm frightened." She shuddered. "Please, Daniel."

He pitied her, but knew what he had to do.

When the ambulance arrived, she didn't put up a fight. Daniel looked into her eyes and knew that the lost look in them would haunt him for the rest of his life. The light had gone out of her. The woman he once knew was gone, and would never return.

The next two years were a nightmare. Becky's mental health deteriorated rapidly, and eventually she had no recollection of Taylor or him. One crisp spring morning, she peacefully died in her sleep. Daniel wondered if at the moment of death she had remembered him or the child they had brought into the world. If she had, did she think he had deserted her and left her to die alone? That was what had disturbed him the most. He mourned the once loving, vibrant woman he'd known. Part of him was relieved that her suffering was finally over, but another part of him yearned for something — anything — that would explain what had happened to her. He would never know when Becky had begun to lose her mind, or if she had always been this way and he'd missed the signs. He'd also wonder whether he could have helped her if he had known. Could he have made a difference?

He ran a hand through his tousled dark brown hair, stood up, and stretched. He walked upstairs to Taylor's room, opened the door, and stood watching her for a few minutes as she slept. A faint smile crossed her lips, and then disappeared as quickly as it had come. He tiptoed over to her and kissed her cheek, then walked back downstairs and into the kitchen to eat the dinner she had prepared.

CHAPTER TWO

The bright morning light cast a glimmering ray over Zoey as she lay sprawled on her back in bed. Squinting against the bright light peeping through the partially opened slats in her window blind, she wanted to sleep a little longer, but knew that she had to get up and prepare for her morning classes. She willed her body to move and then finally rolled to her side and laid there for a few seconds before getting out of bed. The first thing she did was to turn the ringer back on her phone. Last night she had turned it off so she could get some much needed sleep without any distractions. Almost instantaneously, the phone rang. For the first time, Zoey realized how shrill and demanding the sound was to her ears. It rang a second time. She grabbed it before it could assault her senses for the third time.

"Hello," she answered breathlessly.

"Thank God, I finally reached you. Do you know I've been trying to call you since last night? I was worried sick about you. You didn't answer your cell phone or home phone. If you didn't answer this morning I was going to come over to make sure you were okay."

Zoey still wasn't quite awake, and tried to focus on the caller. "Oh, Bella, I'm sorry. I was so tired last night that I just collapsed when I got home. I don't think a bomb could have woke me," she lied. "I left my cell in my bag and turned off the ringer on the land line."

"I'll forgive you this time, my friend. Anyway, I called to remind you that this afternoon we have the fittings for your maid of honor dress and my wedding gown," she said excitedly.

"I'm glad you called...I'd completely forgotten that it was today. What time do we have to be there?"

"Two o'clock. You do remember it's at Rachel's."

"I remember. I may be a few minutes late, but I'll get there as quickly as I can."

"No problem. I'll wait." She paused for a few seconds. "Zoey, is everything okay? You don't seem to be yourself today. Do you want me to come over?"

"No, I'm fine, really. I've got a class this morning, which I'm going to be late for if I don't get a move on. I'll see you at two. I've got to run." She hung up the phone, then looked at her bed, longing to climb back in. She sighed.

The phone rang again. She reluctantly answered it.

"I just wanted to say good morning to the most beautiful woman in the world," a deep voice greeted her tenderly.

Zoey's heartbeat quickened. "Hunter, please stop calling me."

"Is that what you really want?" His voice was passionate.

She hesitated. "You know it's not, but Bella is my best friend. Do you know how I feel every time I see her? Hunter, she's going to be your wife in a few months!"

"But you're the one who has my heart," he answered. "I could never love another woman the way I love you. You know that."

25

Zoey frowned. "I don't think you know what love is," she stated flatly. "If you did, you wouldn't be putting me through this."

"You put yourself in this situation. You weren't forced, now were you? You could have said no, but you didn't. You want me as much as I want you."

Zoey didn't utter a response.

"Just what I thought, baby. We're meant for each other." He chuckled. "I know that I don't want to be with anyone but you. You're on my mind constantly, consuming my every thought."

"Then prove it. Call off the wedding," she said.

"I can't. Imagine what that would do to Bella. Would you really want to crush her like that? Not only would she be losing her fiancé, but her best friend as well."

"She wouldn't have to know about you and me," Zoey insisted. "She wouldn't be losing my friendship."

"So you would still be hiding our relationship. That is no different than what we're doing now. You still wouldn't be able to let her know we're seeing one another."

"Look, Hunter, let's just have a clean break, and Bella will never be the wiser."

"No. I'm not letting you go. I'm going to marry Bella, and you and I will continue on as we have."

"Why marry her? It doesn't make sense. It can't be for her money. What is it, Hunter?"

"Just know that you're the first woman I have ever fallen in love with."

Zoey's head was spinning. "Look, Hunter. I can never undo what I've done to Bella. It makes me sick to my stomach. But I am ending it, and there's nothing you can do about it."

"We're not ending anything, Zoey. Don't forget it."

She inhaled deeply. "I can't deal with this right now, Hunter. I've got a class at ten."

"How about tonight?" he asked. "I want to see you."

"No. It's over. You need to remember that."

"It'll never be over," he said coldly. "Remember that." He clicked off.

Zoey swallowed hard. She threw her clothes on and rushed out of the apartment.

****

Hunter Tucker studied himself in his mirror. He knew that he was well above average in the looks department. Wherever he went, women flocked to him like bees to honey. He wondered if it was his black hair and deep-set midnight blue eyes. Or could it be his deep sexy voice? Maybe it was his muscular body and the way he used his raw sexual appeal to tell a woman exactly what she wanted to hear. He smiled as he continued to gaze at his naked body. Years of working out kept him in top physical condition. He lifted weights every other day, and on the even days ran at the track. His body and looks combined to get him what he wanted out of women.

It never took him long to ease into the graces of some of the wealthiest women in the world. One day he'd marry one of them, and then he'd have the status and prestige he craved. He didn't care about their money. It was the name he wanted to be connected to. He was new money, but they had old money and the honor and respect that went along with it. It couldn't be bought, so he was willing to sacrifice his bachelorhood to worm his way into one of the elite families.

He'd traveled from coast to coast in his quest to find the perfect woman. Most were willing to bed him, but when it came to marriage, they chose to look elsewhere. He knew the real reason was because he didn't meet the criteria from their hard-nosed families. They would bed him, but would marry only into their own kind...those that came from old money. Love didn't seem to factor into it. But then he hadn't loved any of them either.

But when he met Bella Cameron his luck changed. She came from old money, and lots of it, and seemed to be the only one left from her line. A little older than him, she welcomed Hunter into her bed and heart without much effort on his part. Bella had stayed in Vickville, Pennsylvania, where her ancestors had started their lucrative ventures. She stayed out of the business end of things, and was happy to let others handle her vast holdings only making appearances at board meetings when necessary, with her advisors on her arm. It didn't seem to bother her that he was new money. Bella loved him and instantly said yes when he proposed. It would be a perfect union except for one thing. He didn't love her.

He would never forget the night he met her, because that was the night he also met Zoey Davis. He was sitting at the bar of a swanky hotel, toying with his drink, when the most beautiful blonde he had ever seen swept into the room. She was accompanied by an auburn haired woman who was attractive in her own right, but didn't captivate him like the first woman did. He watched as they were escorted to a table.

He recalled how easy it had been to get the women's attention. After he had had an expensive bottle of wine sent to their table, it was only a matter of minutes before they invited him to have a drink with them. He didn't waste any time finding out their current financial standings. Zoey Davis was everything he had ever wanted in a woman, but Bella Cameron had the money.

Hunter smiled smugly as he reached for his razor. There was no way Zoey was going to end anything with him. He wouldn't allow it. He certainly wasn't about to blow everything he'd worked for to gain the status and prestige marrying Bella would afford him. And there was no way he would let go of the only woman he'd ever loved.

****

Daniel looked over his shoulder at the attractive woman making her way to his desk. Her shoulder length dark blonde hair hung loosely over her shoulders, and her red dress clung seductively to her as her hips swayed, while the heels of her shoes made light tapping sounds on the dingy tiled floor.

She reached his desk, her cool blue eyes taking in the immediate surroundings. "Are you Detective Trevors?" she asked in a low voice.

"Yes, I am. What can I do for you?" Daniel asked.

"Are you handling the investigation of the recent stabbing?" She looked hopefully at him.

"Yes, I am. My partner Detective Ben Wilson and I are working with homicide." He studied her carefully, noticing how her bottom lip trembled slightly. "Do you have some information about the case?" He leaned forward in his chair.

"I'm not sure...maybe." She fumbled with the strap of her small purse.

"Please have a seat." He motioned to the chair closest to his desk.

She sat down, nervously clutching her purse. "The news reported that the murders are connected."

"We believe they may be." He studied her. "Did you know one of the victims?"

She drew a shaky breath. "Yes, my brother," she said as her eyes filled with tears.

"Maybe you'd better start at the beginning. What's your

name?" he asked, grabbing paper and pen.

"Stephanie. Stephanie Rinehart."

He was thoughtful for a moment. "Yes, he was the second victim...found on Elmhurst and Wayne."

"I should have contacted you sooner, but I was afraid for my brother's reputation," she said apprehensively.

"Please fill me in, Miss Rinehart," he said, eyeing her carefully.

She drew a deep breath. "Joseph was a good man. He was a hard worker and genuinely a kind person. Everyone who knew him loved him." She took a tissue from her purse and dabbed at her eyes. "But he was hiding something. I knew it. His whole personality started to change. Instead of the kind-hearted man I knew him to be, he became angry and bitter. He started spending money like he was a millionaire. That's when I knew something was wrong. He'd barely made it from check to check, and now he had money to burn. Several times I questioned him about it, but he told me to stay out of his personal business."

"Maybe he had a second job," Daniel offered.

Tears streamed down her face. Daniel handed her a tissue and waited for her to compose herself.

She swallowed hard. "I found out that he did all right." She cleared her throat. "He was a drug runner," she blurted out. "I wish I could have helped him."

Daniel's eyes narrowed. "Can you prove it?" He wondered if she'd had a personal vendetta against her brother to make such an accusation. But her demeanor seemed genuinely crushed by his death.

She nodded. "I followed him one night shortly before he was murdered. He went to the warehouse on the east side...you know the place?"

"Yes, it's been vacant for several years," Daniel answered.

"I parked my car where it wouldn't be seen and sneaked up to the entrance. The door was open a crack, and I saw Joseph talking to another man."

"Did you recognize the other man?"

She shook her head. "I've never seen him before."

"Can you give me a description of him?"

"He's good-looking with a thin mustache, and wears wire-rimmed glasses. He's probably in his mid-thirties. Oh, and his hair is black."

"How was he dressed?"

"Like he was going to a business meeting or something."

"Could you hear their conversation?" Daniel asked.

"At first they were speaking in low voices. I couldn't hear what either of them said. Then Joseph handed the man an envelope. The man looked inside and then took out a stack of bills. He counted the money. He looked at Joseph and accused him of ripping him off. Those were his exact words. Joseph denied it, but the man told him that he had forty-eight hours to either come up with the money or get the drugs back."

"So you believe your brother was running drugs for this guy?"

"Yes. Wouldn't you?" she asked. She didn't wait for a response before continuing. "I didn't want to believe it, but I know what I witnessed with my own two eyes." She wadded the tissue she was holding. "I couldn't believe it! My own brother. The father of two beautiful children, doing something like that!" She dabbed at her eyes again.

"Did you ever confront your brother about what you had seen?" Daniel asked.

"Yes, I did. He pleaded with me not to tell anyone." Her voice softened. "He wanted to provide the best for his family, and he just couldn't make it on his salary. He was old-fashioned and didn't want his wife to work. He wanted her home to take care of the kids. I told him that the money he was making selling drugs was illegal and would never make him happy, but he refused to listen to me. He was breaking the law, and I warned him that if he was caught, he'd go to prison and his family would have nothing at all."

"Do you know how long he was involved in it?"

"No, I don't know. It must have been at least six months, though, since that's when I noticed his personality change. He never told me...that's just my guess." She bit her bottom lip. "I disowned him as my brother the night I confronted him. A few days later he was murdered." Her voice trembled, and then broke. "If I had only gone to the police with this information he might be alive today. Maybe he'd be in prison, but he'd be alive! I blame myself, and I will have to live with it for the rest of my life," she sobbed.

Daniel gave her a few minutes to compose herself before speaking. "Would you be willing to sign a formal statement testifying to everything you've just told me?" he asked.

"Yes. I'll do whatever I can to get that bastard off the streets."

****

Bella Cameron peered out of the dress shop window. It was already half past two, and Zoey was nowhere in sight. She frowned. It did no good to complain, because Zoey had been this way ever since they had met and become friends in junior high school. She should have told Zoey to be there at one o'clock, and then maybe she would have been on time. No matter what, Bella could never stay mad at her.

Bella had been raised as a pampered little princess, and after much pleading, had been allowed, against her parents' better judgment, to attend the local junior high school instead of being sent to a boarding school. She had almost regretted her decision until Zoey Davis befriended her and took her under her wing. Zoey was out-going, independent, energetic, and fun loving, the exact opposite of Bella. Gradually though, Zoey had managed to bring Bella out of her shell. Bella's happiness had always been bought for her, but Zoey showed her the things that money could never buy.

Bella held a dress against her thin frame as she daydreamed about her fiancé. The night she had met Hunter she was certain that he would bypass her for Zoey. It always happened that way, even though Zoey never encouraged it. She just had a charisma that naturally attracted men to her. But that night Zoey had excused herself from the table to give Bella a chance to speak alone with Hunter. Bella would be forever grateful to her for that courtesy. Bella had not only been captivated by Hunter Tucker's looks, but also by his genuine interest in knowing everything about her and her family background. When the night had come to an end, she had secured a date with him for the following evening.

A hand gently squeezed her shoulder, startling her back to the present.

"What were you thinking?"

"Hunter!" She threw her arms around his neck. "What are you doing here?"

"Just making sure everything is under control." He kissed her cheek. "Now, tell me, what has you so starry-eyed?"

She smiled up at him. "As if you didn't know." She looked at the clock. "I hope that Zoey didn't forget that she's supposed to meet me here. She's always running late, but this is late even for her. "

Before the sentence was even finished, Zoey came bursting through the door. "Sorry I'm late," she called breathlessly.

"Nice to see you, Zoey." Hunter smiled. He kissed her cheek. "I'd better let you two attend to your business." He drew Bella to him. Her back faced Zoey, and Hunter made a play to passionately kiss his bride to be as he winked at Zoey.

Zoey threw him a warning look as she turned to the dress the fitter had left on the rack for her. She took the dress and delicately held it up while Bella and Hunter said their goodbyes. Her heart pumped irregularly as she felt the sharpness of Hunter's eyes on her back. His eyes seemed to be boring through to her very soul, and she knew that the kisses he so freely gave to Bella could never match the passion she shared with him. She felt her face flush, and said, "I'm going to try my dress on." Once inside the dressing room, she leaned against the wall to steady her trembling legs. The wall felt cool against her hot flesh.

"Let me help you try it on," Bella smiled as she entered the cubicle seconds later. She took the dress from Zoey's hands. "This is beautiful, Zoey. Monica designed it exactly as we wanted."

"Yes, she did," Zoey replied.

"Are you okay?" Bella asked. "You're trembling."

Zoey gave her a faint smile. "Just a little dizzy...I skipped lunch."

Bella looked closely at her, but said nothing.

****

Taylor sat cross-legged on her bed. "What shade of eye shadow should I use?" She turned to her friend.

"I think the blue looks best," Sara Kane answered. She stood in front of the mirror trying on a pair of earrings. "How do these look?" she asked, turning from the mirror to look at Taylor.

"Great. You can borrow them if you want to."

"Thanks. I think I will."

"I wish I could go to the party Saturday night," Taylor said. "Everybody's going to be there."

"So go," Sara replied with a slight shrug of her thin shoulders. "Tell your father you're going to a friend's house."

Sara frowned. "No. I wouldn't feel right sneaking out behind his back."

"He'd never find out."

Taylor sighed. "No. I can't lie to him."

"Well, I don't have to worry about answering to anyone." Sara laughed bitterly. "Because no one in my family gives a damn about me."

"That's not true, Sara, and you know it. They care about you."

"I'm not talking about Randy and Andy. My parents couldn't care less about any of us. I don't remember the last time either of them asked me or my brothers where we were going or when we'd be home." She shrugged. "So, I go where I want to and do what I want to."

"Come on, Sara, your parents care about what happens to you and your brothers."

She flopped down on Taylor's bed and rolled onto her stomach, propping her chin up on her hands. "I used to hope and pray that they did, but I know it's just not so. When I walk out the door, no one cares where I go or if I ever come back," she retorted. "I could go missing and they'd never know it."

****

Out of the corner of her eye, Zoey spotted Hunter staring at her. "Finish your warm up exercises and I'll be right back," she instructed her students. She grabbed her towel and rushed breathlessly to the restroom, where she knew he would be waiting for her.

Hunter smiled appreciatively at her as his eyes hungrily took in her body. He pulled her into the restroom and shut and locked the door.

"What are you doing here?" she demanded.

"After seeing you today, I couldn't stay away. I need you now." He nuzzled her neck with his lips. "I know you want it, too."

"Hunter, I want you to leave."

He smiled. "I don't think you really do." He stared into her eyes.

She placed her hands on his chest, pushing him away from her. "Hunter, go...I've got work to do," she said firmly. "I've got to get back to my class."

"Come on," he pleaded. He reached for her.

"No!" she stated firmly. "I'm not doing this anymore. Get that through your head. How many times do I have to tell you that? What we had, or thought we had, is over."

He looked intently at her. "I don't believe you." He continued looking at her and then smirked. "Out of the blue you want to end it between us? Your body language tells me something different."

"That's your imagination." She placed her hand on the doorknob. "I told you I don't feel right about what we've been doing."

"What we've been doing?" he said with a slight laugh.

"You know what I mean. My God, Hunter. I can't believe I've sunk this low. I should have never allowed this to happen. And if you had a heart, you wouldn't marry Bella. How can you hurt her like that?"

He raised his eyebrows. "Don't tell me I'm going to get a lecture on morals, from you of all people," he said sarcastically.

Her eyes narrowed. "I feel cheap and dirty for what I've done to her. I can't keep hurting her like this. It needs to end."

"But she doesn't know about us."

"And I don't want to risk her ever finding out."

"We'll just have to be more careful. Especially after the wedding. She knows I travel for business, so I can tell her I'm on a business trip and that will give us time together."

Zoey's forehead furrowed. "If you love me so much then why are you marrying her?"

He threw his head back and laughed. "Are you paranoid? Is that what you're fishing for? You want a marriage proposal?"

"No, not from you Hunter. Not anymore. Maybe I did before, but not anymore."

"Do you even know what you want, Zoey? You have a restless spirit. I think you love the way your adrenalin pumps when we sneak around to be together. That's what excites you."

Her eyes narrowed. "What I want is to turn back time to before the night I met you. If only I could. I never realized how perfect my life was. I had everything. Most importantly, I had a man who truly loved me and wanted a future with me."

"With Daniel?" He snickered. "I doubt he even knows how to handle a woman like you."

"What's that supposed to mean?"

"You know exactly what it means," he said, placing a hand on her arm. "You're a very passionate woman."

She shook his hand off. "Don't touch me, Hunter. I want you out of my life once and for all. I'm tired of your games. What will it take to convince you to stay away from me?"

His jaw tightened. "I never forced you into anything. If you cared about Bella as much as you proclaim, you wouldn't have gotten involved with me in the first place. You threw your friendship with her away the minute you jumped into bed with me."

Zoey couldn't deny what he said. Sure, she could say she had a moment of weakness and fell for his charisma, but deep down she knew it still would never excuse the betrayal to the two people who'd meant everything in the world to her.

"If Daniel had meant so much to you, you wouldn't have cheated on him," Hunter said. "So obviously you've been deluding yourself."

She looked into his eyes. "I'll regret that until the day I die. I had to break off with him because I couldn't stand myself. He deserves so much better."

"It's too late to turn back time. And I don't think you really regret the passion we shared. Maybe what's really bothering you...you can't stand the fact that Bella will be in my bed every night instead of you."

"I really feel sorry for Bella. She loves you and you couldn't care less about her. There's nothing more to say, Hunter. Just go." She ran a hand through her hair.

He leaned in close. "You'll never be rid of me, babe," he whispered. "I told you that." He put his hand over hers, which was still on the doorknob, opened the door, and then left without another word.

Zoey leaned against the cool, tiled wall of the small room for a few seconds. She'd have time to process everything later, but right now she had to get back to her students.

****

Taylor removed the pizza from the oven.

"I'll cut it," Sara offered.

Taylor handed the pizza cutter to her. "Did you go to the party the other night?"

"Yeah. Asher and I stopped in for a little while, but we didn't stay too long. It was dull."

"Meg called and said the same thing. So I guess I didn't miss much."

"Not at all." Sara grinned. "Except when Meg put Caleb in his place. Asher and I were leaving and we saw them outside, but they didn't see us. They were arguing."

"Meg never mentioned anything to me. They've only been going out for a couple of weeks. I'm sure they must have made up." She squinted. "I wonder why she didn't mention it, though."

Sara shrugged. "I don't know. He was trying to convince her to have sex."

"I doubt she did. Guys want to rush into everything."

Sara stopped cutting the pizza. "Yeah, I know what you mean." Her dark hair glistened under the bright kitchen light. "Asher expected everything on our first date."

Taylor noticed Sara's face reddening. "You didn't, did you?" Her eyes grew wide.

"Of course not." She looked at Taylor. "I wanted to, but something inside wouldn't let me." She chewed on her bottom lip. "You know what really gets me?" she continued. "It's the kids at school. They think I've given out to every guy I've dated! You don't know how it feels to be accused of something you didn't do," she said bitterly. "I hate my life. You don't know what it's like in my family."

Taylor frowned as she looked at her friend, studying Sara's features. Sara's long, black hair hung loosely against her small-boned frame, making her look almost fragile. Her skin was fair and flawless, and she had high cheekbones and dark eyes perfectly spaced in her beautiful face. She constantly flirted with the boys at school, even going out with a couple of seniors, and soon got a reputation for being easy.

39

"Sara, is your life really that bad? You have a mother and father, and you have your brothers. My life hasn't always been easy either. Nobody has a perfect life."

"Give me a break, Taylor! It's not just that. It's the way the girls at school talk about me behind my back."

Taylor fumbled for the right words. "They say that because of the way you act around the boys. You did date a lot of them."

"That doesn't mean I had sex with them! It's just harmless flirting." Sara looked into Taylor's eyes. "You don't believe me! You are my best friend and you don't believe me." Tears stung her eyes. "I really thought you would have my back, Taylor. I guess I was wrong. Thanks a lot!" She threw the pizza cutter on the counter, grabbed her jacket, and slipped it on.

"Come on, Sara, I believe you," Taylor said. "I know those boys were just talking, and the girls are probably just jealous. And, yes, I know your life has been rough. I was just trying to explain that nobody really knows what anyone's life is really like. It just came out wrong."

"Yeah, right!" She hastily zipped her jacket.

"Where are you going?"

"None of your business!" She rushed out of the kitchen door before Taylor could say another word.

Taylor slumped into a chair. Why did everything always end up in a mess when all she ever wanted to do was help? She never wanted to be the cause of anyone's pain, especially her best friend's. She was so wrapped up in her thoughts that she didn't hear her father enter the kitchen a few minutes later.

"What's the matter, Princess?" Daniel asked, planting a kiss on top of her head. "You look like you've just lost your best friend."

"I think I have." She bit her bottom lip. "Sara's mad at me.

She was supposed to spend the night, but she left."

"Want to talk about it?" Daniel asked.

Taylor slowly lifted her head. "Dad, why does life have to be so hard? Sometimes it seems like no matter how hard you try, it just keeps getting more complicated and messed up."

Daniel pulled up a chair and sat down next to her. He took her small hand in his. "What happened?"

"I hurt her feelings without meaning to." Her eyes widened. "Dad, she's my best friend. I would never deliberately hurt her. I was only trying to help her."

"Is she in some kind of trouble, Taylor?"

She shook her head. "No, just some kids at school saying things about her. She thought I agreed with them and doesn't believe that I don't."

"Is she being bullied?"

"No. They haven't made threats or anything. They're saying things about her because she was hanging out with some of the girls' boyfriends."

"Let me know if anything escalates."

"I will, but I don't think it'll go any further than the gossip, Dad."

"Okay." Daniel was thoughtful for a minute. "Give her time to cool off, Taylor. She'll come around in a day or two."

"I wish I could be sure."

He smiled. "Take your old man's word for it."

"I suppose," she replied, even though it didn't make her feel better.

He looked at the uneaten pizza. "Why don't you warm that up and I'll grab a quick shower."

"Okay, Dad." She stood up just as the phone rang. "I've got it," she said. "Maybe it's Sara."

Daniel winked at her with an I-told-you-so look in his eyes. Taylor smiled as she picked up the phone. "Hello." She paused. "Just a sec. I'll get him. It's for you," she said, holding the phone out to her father. "It's Zoey."

Daniel raised his eyebrows as he took the phone. "Is something wrong, Zoey?"

Taylor couldn't help but hear her father's end of the conversation. She wished things had worked out for them. She'd been a student of Zoey Davis's for a couple of years and had been overjoyed when her father and Zoey had begun dating. She liked Zoey. She was the only woman Daniel had dated since her mother's death that she'd felt comfortable with. She had been heartbroken, as much for herself as she was for her father, when their relationship had ended.

She wished she could hear what Zoey was saying. She couldn't read anything in her father's expression, but his eyes seemed brighter. She often wondered why Zoey and her father had quit seeing each other. She saw the deep hurt and pain in his eyes whenever Zoey's name was mentioned, and figured that Zoey had ended things, not him.

****

"No, Daniel." Her voice was soft and low. "I've just been thinking that I owe you an explanation about why I broke off so abruptly with you."

"No, you don't owe me anything," he answered. "You made your feelings perfectly clear. We want different things. Maybe a different time or different place, but the timing was off for us."

"Daniel, could we meet to talk?" Zoey asked.

"I don't think that's a good idea, Zoey."

"Please don't make this difficult for me, Daniel," Zoey said. "I was wrong. I've been thinking about you ever since you stopped by the studio." She drew a deep breath. "I don't want it to be over between us. I know I hurt you terribly. I'm asking for another chance."

"What brought about this sudden change of heart?" His eyes narrowed.

"I miss you, Daniel."

He hesitated for a moment as he shrugged his shoulders at Taylor. "The other day at your studio you didn't act like it."

"Can we at least get together to talk?"

"Okay. Would you like to have dinner tomorrow?" Daniel asked.

"Would seven be okay?" Zoey asked.

"I'll pick you up at your apartment." He hung up the phone and turned to Taylor, who was busy setting the table.

"So?" she asked looking at him.

"I'm taking Zoey to dinner tomorrow night."

Taylor grinned. "Does this mean you two are getting back together?"

He held a hand up palm out. "It's just dinner. Don't go reading anything more into it."

"Sure, Dad," she said.

****

Zoey hung up the phone. She'd accomplished the first part of her plan. She knew that Daniel still cared about her, and she did care about him. She always would. Getting him to see her again would be the easy part. The hard part would be convincing Hunter that she was through with him for good. But she still loved him. He was a cold, calculating, heartless man. The complete opposite of Daniel. She loved both men but in different ways, ways that were as different as they each were. She knew it was crazy. Her heart would always yearn for Hunter, even though she had to let

43

him go for both their sakes.

She picked up a magazine and thumbed through it, but couldn't concentrate, so tossed it aside. Her head was throbbing and she felt hot tears building behind her eyelids. She'd brought this mess on herself, and knew there was no way out without those she cared about most in this world being hurt. Her pain was something she knew she deserved. No one had forced her to do the deceitful things she had. She didn't expect forgiveness, and doubted any would be forthcoming. She swallowed the lump in her throat, walked into her small kitchen, and fixed a cup of tea.

She carried her tea into the living room, set it down to cool, then picked the magazine up again. Her hands started to shake at the same time the tears she had been fighting splashed down her cheeks. Her heart and soul ached for Hunter. She hated herself for wanting him. These emotions made her feel powerless. She had always been in charge of her emotions...that was until she met Hunter. He had such a powerful control over her that it consumed her. She couldn't understand why he had such a hold over her. She felt like she was drowning, and there was no hope of survival.

How could Hunter profess his love for her and at the same time plan to marry someone else? How dare he expect her to be his mistress, when he would be sharing his bed every night with her best friend? Her mind could not cope with all this pressure. For too long, guilt had wracked her. She could never expect Bella to forgive her or even to understand. Hunter was using both of them. She wanted to hate him for emotionally destroying her, but couldn't. Why couldn't she hate him?

She wouldn't think twice about giving up her own life to spare his. But she doubted that he would do the same for her. His love for her was not strong enough, or he would end his relationship with Bella. Now anger began to build. "Damn you, Hunter!" she shouted. "Why can't I get you out of my system?" The tears now fell free and heavy, and she was unable to control them.

Something inside of her was dying. Her heart was twisting, crumbling, and slowly being torn to shreds. It would never be the same. Life would continue, but she would just exist. That's all that was left for her now. She didn't want to hurt Daniel again...he didn't deserve it. But as soon as Bella and Hunter were comfortably settled into their marriage, she would end it with him once again. This time it would be final. He would be hurt, but it was the only way she knew to protect him. Daniel deserved to find someone who would return his love unconditionally, but that woman could never be her. She wouldn't be able to live with him knowing that she shared her love with another man. She'd rather spend the rest of her life alone then bring him deeper into her tangled web. Even if there were a way to be certain that Daniel would never find out about Hunter, she would never be happy with deceiving him.

As far as Bella was concerned, it was unbearable seeing her joy and happiness when she knew it was all a con on Hunter's part. She'd have to figure out a way to ease herself out of Bella's life. That wouldn't be easy either, but she couldn't stand what she'd done to her best friend and watching Hunter play the part of the attentive doting husband. If only she'd never succumbed to Hunter in the first place she wouldn't be in this mess. She'd been happy with Daniel, and believed she was destined to spend the rest of her life with him. Now that was destroyed. She covered her face with her hands as her mind swept her into her own personal hell of emotions.

****

Hunter Tucker combed his hair, and then looked around his room for a clean shirt, finally settling on a light blue one to go with his gray slacks. He tossed a sport coat on his unmade bed and then stood, smiling at the bed. It was too large for the room, actually taking up the bulk of it. He sighed deeply, recalling the passion that had taken place between him and Zoey on that bed. Zoey could tell him a thousand times that she never wanted to see him again, but her heart told him otherwise. After their first torrid night together, no man would ever again be able to satisfy her in bed.

He would make sure that Bella never found out about Zoey, but if she ever did, he had that figured out, too. Bella would be crushed that her best friend had seduced him, but she would forgive him for succumbing to Zoey's charms. After all, what man could resist Zoey Davis? Bella was crazy about him and would never leave him — of that he had no doubt — but she could never match Zoey's hot, raw hunger in bed. Bella was secure in his love...he had worked hard to make her feel secure.

Hunter picked up his sport coat, slipped it on, and then admired himself in the mirror. He checked the time, and then quietly left his room.

****

Daniel stood by the coffee maker waiting for the pot to fill. He turned his head when his partner appeared at his side holding a cup in his hand. "It'll be ready in a minute."

"What do you think of Stephanie Rinehart's statement?" Ben Wilson asked.

Daniel frowned. "I think she's telling the truth about what she saw, but something just doesn't click. If we could only get a better composite of the man she said met her brother."

Ben's eyes narrowed. "At least we know he's well-dressed.

So he's obviously someone with money and power."

"True," Daniel replied as he took Ben's cup and poured the coffee. "That could be almost anybody in this city." He handed the cup to Ben. "If she could only think of something else, like a tattoo, a scar, anything to set him apart from everyone else."

"Even if she did, that still doesn't mean that he's our murderer."

Daniel added sugar to his coffee. "No, it doesn't, but it doesn't mean he's not, either." He sipped his coffee. "I only hope that Stephanie can give us what we need before we're looking at another crime scene."

Ben frowned. "I can't even come up with a decent hunch on this one. I usually get a deep gut feeling." He looked at Daniel. "But nothing this time."

Daniel took another sip of coffee. "I know what you mean. But we'll get him, Ben. Whether it's the same man Stephanie Rinehart described or someone else. He's bound to slip up." His voice was firm. "I guarantee you that we'll get him."

Ben shook his head, and then rubbed his eyes. "I only hope it's before he strikes again."

Daniel eyed him warily. "You seem distracted. Everything okay, Ben?"

He frowned again. "Yeah. Except that Clare wants a couple hundred more a month." He laughed bitterly. "That woman's bleeding me dry. She's already taken everything."

"Can't your lawyer help?"

"Nah. It's called keeping up with inflation. The older Josh gets, the more money she needs to provide for him." His jaw hardened. "It wouldn't be so bad if I got to see him once in a while. It's hard to maintain any kind of normal relationship with him with only a couple of phone calls a month. Just once, I'd like to be there to watch him in a baseball game."

Daniel wished he could say something to ease Ben's distress. He'd never been in this kind of situation, but knew the toll it was taking on his partner. Ben was a good father, and nothing was too good for his son. To have your child pulled abruptly from your life was something he couldn't even imagine.

Chapter Three

Hunter took Bella's elbow as they were led to their table. He gently pulled her chair out, seated her, and then seated himself. After ordering their drinks, he picked up a menu. "What are you in the mood for?" he asked.

"I'm not sure," Bella answered as she studied the menu for a couple of minutes. "Hunter, is everything okay?" Before he could respond, their drinks arrived. Bella waited until the waiter had gone before speaking again. "Are you feeling all right tonight, Hunter? You were very quiet on the drive over."

"I'm fine." He flashed her a quick smile. "Just business." He patted her hand. "Now don't you go worrying about me."

She frowned. "It comes with the territory." She lifted an eyebrow as she peered at him. "I want to help. If you're having financial problems, please let me know, Hunter."

He inhaled deeply. "Bella, I'm not having financial problems. I don't know where you get that. One of my investments is having a few problems, but it'll get worked out. It happens all the time, and is definitely nothing that would affect my personal financial stability. My investments are well protected."

She lowered her eyes and looked at her menu again.

"Honey, I'm sorry if I've hurt your feelings. That is not my intention." His voice was soft. "I appreciate your offer to help, but I don't need it. I'm fine." He picked up her hand and gently caressed it. "Do you know how much I love you?" He stared into her eyes.

She smiled. "Yes, but I love hearing you tell me."

****

Zoey turned the music up. "All right, girls!" she said loudly, clapping her hands. "Let's go through the routine one more time! I want it perfect this time!" She kept her eye on Taylor Trevors. She knew Taylor well enough to know that Taylor's mind was definitely not on the dance routine. Normally Taylor was a perfectionist, but Zoey noticed how even the simplest routine today seemed to throw her off. She caught Taylor's eye and the teen looked away, embarrassed.

When the routine was over and the other girls were heading to the changing room, she walked up to Taylor. She wondered if the teen was worried about Daniel and her getting together for dinner. She'd always gotten along with Taylor, even after Daniel and she had gone their separate ways, but possibly Taylor was afraid that her father would be hurt again. She wanted to reach out to her like she had in the past. Taylor and she had spent hours shopping and talking about everything under the sun. She missed those times. She wanted them back, but knew she had to take her time. Taylor may not be so quick to share with her as she once had been. Maybe they'd never have that tight bond again. Her heart squeezed. Taylor had looked up to her like a mother, and she'd thought of Taylor as a daughter. Again, she'd thrown away everything for a man who put his own needs above anyone else's. But she needed to let Taylor know she was there for her.

She'd take it one step at a time.

Taylor looked up at her. "Hi," she said with a bright smile.

Zoey returned her smile. "How's everything going?" she asked gently.

"Great! Sorry about messing up the routine."

"Don't worry about it. You're entitled to an off day." She sensed that the teen wanted to say more. Taylor's eyes searched hers for a few seconds, but she kept silent. Zoey placed a hand on Taylor's shoulder. "If you ever need to talk, you know that you can come to me."

"I know," she answered with the same bright smile. "Thanks."

****

Daniel studied Zoey's long slender legs. He longed to run his hand up and down her smooth flesh. He took a deep breath and tried to focus on Zoey's face, but that was easier said than done. She crossed her legs and leaned forward in the easy chair adjacent to where he sat on the matching sofa. His eyes moved back down to her legs. He swallowed hard, imagining his lips kissing her full sensuous lips while his hands caressed her firm perky breasts. He missed those times. No, he had to forget the past. He wouldn't allow himself to be hurt again. Zoey Davis couldn't just waltz in and out of his life whenever she wanted to, no matter how much he yearned for her. He had to be strong and fight his urges, but he knew he was only kidding himself. If she made a move, he'd take her back in a heartbeat. She had a hold on him that he couldn't shake no matter how hard he tried. He straightened his shoulders and focused on a decorative plaque on the wall above Zoey's head.

"Is something wrong, Daniel?" she asked softly.

His face flushed. "No, everything's fine. I guess my mind wandered for a moment." He picked up his coffee cup. "I was

51

surprised when you called."

She studied him for a minute. "I didn't know how much I missed you until you stopped at the studio, Daniel." She twisted her hands together.

Daniel wanted to leap up and take her in his arms, but he kept quiet as he looked into her eyes.

"Would you care for anything else?"

"No, thanks." He set the cup down, and then leaned back into the sofa. "I missed you, too, Zoey. Your phone call last night took me by surprise."

"I never meant to hurt you, Daniel." Her bottom lip trembled slightly. "I was afraid. Things were moving too fast for me. I should have talked to you instead of running from you."

"And now?" he asked.

"Daniel, I never stopped loving you." She swallowed hard. "If you're willing, I want to give us another chance."

He wanted to believe her. He needed to believe her. "We had some good times."

She nodded. "We did. I treasure every one of them. I've relived them over and over."

He rubbed his jaw. "I want to give us another chance, too." He watched as she rose and walked toward him.

She sat next to him and took his hand. "Daniel, I'm sorry for hurting you."

He rubbed his thumb over her hand. "Let's make a fresh start, Zoey."

Tears sprang to her eyes. "Thank you."

He drew her into his arms and kissed her.

****

Zoey couldn't bear for Daniel to be hurt again, but he would be and he didn't deserve it. There was no other way. She fought back hot tears and squeezed her eyes shut as she rested her head against his strong chest, listening to the rhythmic beating of his heart…a heart that she would break again. She hated herself for what she was doing to him, and she hated herself for what she had let Hunter do to her.

He held her tightly and didn't see the tear that escaped and silently slid down her cheek.

****

Asher took a sack from the pouch attached to his motorcycle.

"Where are we, Asher? I can't see a thing," Sara said. She shivered. "Besides being dark, it's cold here, too." She rubbed her hands together.

"I'll warm you up." He took her hand. "Come on. I want to show you something."

Sara hesitated. "I don't know. Maybe we should go to our usual spot. There's no one around here," she said nervously.

"That's the point. We have total privacy."

"It's creepy here. It reminds me of one of those horror movies." She shivered again.

"Come on. There's nothing to be afraid of. Wait till you see this spot I found."

He tugged at her hand and she reluctantly walked next to him, careful of every step she took. A gentle breeze rippled the leaves on a nearby tree while the moon played peek-a-boo between the branches. A twig snapped under Asher's feet, causing Sara to jump.

"What was that?" she asked, holding tight to his arm.

He laughed. "Just a twig. Nothing to worry about. It's peaceful here, Sara. Why do you need a bunch of people around you? Don't you trust me?" His voice was gentle.

She heard the disappointment in his voice and felt guilty that she had hurt his feelings. She loved him so much. "Yes, Asher, I trust you." She held tightly to his hand. "What do you want to show me?" She tried to make her voice light.

He squeezed her hand as he led her down a path to the edge of a lake. The moonlight glistened over the water, making it look like diamonds sparkling. She sucked her breath in. "This is beautiful, Asher."

Asher grinned. "I knew you'd like it." He took off his jacket and spread it on the ground. "Come on, sit down," he said. He opened the sack and took out two cans of beer, pulled the tabs off, handed one to her, and took a large swallow from his own. After a few minutes, he pulled a bottle from his jacket pocket, carefully opened it, and then took a large gulp. "Here," he offered. "This stuff is really good. A friend of mine got it for me."

Sara shook her head. "No, Asher, beer is enough for me, and I've already had enough of that for one night." She looked cautiously at the bottle he held in his hand. "Please don't drink any more. If you get busted, you'll lose your bike. And your father will kill you."

He grinned. "I won't get busted. You worry too much, Sara. Loosen up." He slid closer to her and threw an arm around her shoulders. "We've been going together for quite awhile now."

"We have," she answered.

"Now the question is, where do we go from here?"

Sara frowned. "We just keep going out like always."

He planted soft kisses on her neck. "Maybe we need to take the next step."

Shivers ran up and down her spine. He kissed her lips as his large hands caressed her back, then moved to her breasts. His touches felt wonderful and she didn't want them to stop, but she knew she had to stop him before they went too far. She slapped his hands away. Asher didn't stop. He pulled at her clothes. "Stop it!" She pushed away from him. "You know I won't do it with you, Asher."

His eyes narrowed. "If you really love me you will. Or maybe you don't love me."

"If you cared about me, Asher, you wouldn't want me to do something I'm not ready for." She glanced around, knowing there was no one within miles. They were in total seclusion, but even though she was nervous, she still knew Asher wouldn't force himself on her. The wind picked up, warning of an approaching storm. "Let's go before it starts raining."

He grabbed her wrist roughly. With his other hand, he took another swallow from the bottle. "Hey, what's the big deal anyway? Everybody thinks we're doing it." His voice was sarcastic. "Besides, it's a well-known fact around school that you slept with a couple of guys."

"I never did!" she said. "They're only rumors."

"I saw the way you acted around them."

She shook her head. "I never did anything with them. I only flirted with them to piss off their girlfriends who were giving me a rough time. It was stupid. But I swear nothing happened."

His eyes slanted. "I'm not so sure about that. Why would everybody think you did?"

"I don't care what anybody thinks." She looked into his eyes.

"The guys you supposedly only flirted with tell a different story."

"They're lying." She tried to pull her wrist free. "Let go of me."

"You know you want it as much as I do," he insisted.

"No, not like this, Asher," she said firmly. "I'm sure Randy and Andy won't be very happy when I tell them what you tried to do tonight."

"Hell, they won't care. They probably think I'm already getting it from you." He smirked at her.

Sara was surprised at Asher's attitude. This wasn't like him, and for the first time since they'd met, Sara was afraid of him. "That's not true, Asher. And if you believe that then you don't know them as well as you think. You're drunk and don't know what you're saying." She bit her bottom lip. "Don't you remember our talks when we first met? You said you were glad that there were still some girls with morals. You wanted a girlfriend who hadn't slept around."

He snickered. "Guys say that all the time, Sara. Do you really think we mean it? Besides, do you know how ridiculous that sounds? Especially coming from you? Face it, you have a rep." He tossed the bottle to the ground.

His words stung. "I told you I don't care what you or anyone says or thinks, Asher. I want to wait until I get married." Tears filled her eyes. "Can't you understand that, Asher?"

"The only thing I understand, Sara, is that I want what everyone thinks I'm already getting." He tugged at her jeans. "Come on, you know you really want it, too."

"Not like this, Asher."

His eyes were glassy. He grabbed both of her wrists. "You want it as much as I do," he insisted.

She smelled the whiskey on his breath and gagged. She had to make a move and make it quick. She looked into his eyes and then brought her knee up, but missed his crotch.

Asher yelped as he grabbed his stomach. "What's wrong with you?" he demanded angrily. "Who needs you? You're nothing but cheap trash! You strut it around like it's worth a million bucks." He grabbed the sack. "You're not worth it." His eyes darkened. "Fuck you!" He walked toward the path. "Come on if you want a ride home."

****

Taylor opened the door, and was surprised to see Sara standing on the other side. "Hi, Sara. I'm glad you came over." She lifted an eyebrow. "I hope this means that you're not mad at me anymore."

"Would I be here if I was?" she asked in a husky voice as she leaned unsteadily against the open door. "Well, you gonna let me in or what?"

"Sure." Taylor stood aside as Sara made her way into the room. "Take off your jacket. You're dripping."

Sara removed her jacket and handed it to Taylor. "Where's your dad?" she asked, quickly looking around the living room. "Is he here?"

"He's out. I think Zoey and him might be getting back together." She walked closer to Sara, noticing the bruises on her wrists. "What happened to your wrists?"

"Nothing." She lowered her eyes.

Taylor looked at her warily as she led her to the sofa. "Did something happen to you?"

"I said no." She sighed heavily. "You want a beer? I can get us some."

"No. How much have you had tonight, Sara?"

She shrugged. "Just a couple with Asher."

"Where is he?"

"How the hell do I know? He doesn't answer to me."

"You know he has a bad reputation."

Her eyes flamed as she glared at Taylor. "You mean like me? Don't believe everything you hear, Taylor. Maybe you should try to get to know someone before believing lies about them."

"I never said I believed the rumors about you."

"Right. Your actions speak louder than words. I didn't see you picking up the phone to call me."

Taylor frowned. Sara was drunk and it bothered her, especially since both of Sara's parents were alcoholics.

Sara put her feet on the coffee table.

"Please put your feet down, Sara. I just dusted, and besides, you might scratch it up with your shoes."

Sara brought her feet to the floor, scraping the table with her heels. "Oh, *excuse* me. I certainly wouldn't want to ruin any of your precious things," she said sarcastically. "Maybe I should just take off. I don't know why I came here anyway."

"What's your problem, Sara?" Her eyes narrowed. "I never did anything to you."

Sara shook her head. "Must be nice to live in such a fancy house."

Taylor glanced around the living room. The furnishings were nice, but not expensive. The most valuable furnishings in the room were two antique bookcases, which her father had inherited from his parents. He had spent many painstaking hours restoring them to their natural beauty. Taylor knew that he'd worked hard for everything they owned.

Sara slowly let her breath out as she stared at Taylor. "You are afraid to go out and have fun. I don't know why I even bother hanging around with you."

Taylor blinked. "No, I'm not. Our ideas of fun differ. And if you don't want to be friends with me, then that's your choice. I do have other friends." She stared at Sara. "Why did you come here? To insult me? Why don't you just leave and go find Asher?" She drew a deep breath. "You're drunk. If you could only see yourself, you would realize how disgusting you're acting," she replied angrily.

"What do you care anyway?" Sara asked as she slowly stood up, and then wavered on unbalanced legs. "Nobody gives a shit about me."

"What's the matter with you? I *do* care. A lot of people care, but you won't let anyone get close to you. You've had a rough life, big deal...so have I. Quit blaming the world and start fighting back. You can be anything you want to be, but you have to want it bad enough! So what if you fall on your face? We all do. Why don't you start taking control of your life? All you do is complain about everything and everybody." She wagged a finger at her. "I treat you like the sister I don't have, and that still is not good enough." She shook her head. "I don't care anymore, Sara. The next time you get messed up, find someone else to run to."

Sara tried to steady herself, but fell back onto the sofa. She rubbed her temples. "I'm sorry, Taylor." Her bottom lip quivered. "You're right."

Taylor walked over to her. "Tell me what's going on. Why are you doing this to yourself? Why did you drink so much? I've never seen you drunk, and it scares me."

Sara looked into her eyes. "I don't know what happened. Tonight was so messed up. Asher and I had a fight, but you wouldn't understand. I love him...I really do." She gulped. "He wanted me to prove that I loved him."

Taylor's eyes widened. "Oh God, Sara, you didn't!"

"He insisted. He was drunk and moving too fast. His hands were all over me." She started to cry. "I...I pushed him away. He called me names and said he never wanted to see me again." She sniffed. "He pushed me around a little." She lifted her wrists. "That's how the bruises happened." She looked at Taylor. "But I didn't let him touch me. He was acting so odd tonight." She covered her face with her hands. "I don't know what to do."

Taylor sat next to her and put her arms around her. "It'll be all right, Sara. At least you didn't give in to him. Don't you see what that means? You said no."

"But I love him, Taylor. He's the only person, besides you and my brothers, who gives a damn about me."

Taylor gave her a tissue. "Let things cool down for a few days," she said, using the advice her father had given her.

She blew her nose. "I don't know why I constantly screw up." She brushed the matted hair from her forehead. "I wish I wouldn't have drank all that beer tonight." She gagged. "I think I'm going to be sick," she mumbled.

"Come on," Taylor said, grabbing her arm and leading her to the bathroom. She held Sara's hair back and then looked at the tiled wall as her own stomach heaved while Sara threw up. Taylor smelled the faint pine cleaner which she had used earlier to scrub the room. She swallowed hard, choking back the bile, which rose in her own throat as the pine fumes, mixed with the odor of Sara's vomit, assaulted her nostrils. Taylor hoped Sara would remember this the next time she picked up a drink.

The front door opened and seconds later closed. "That's my dad," she whispered to Sara.

"Taylor? I'm home." Daniel called.

"In the bathroom, Dad. I'll be right out," Taylor called back. "I'll be right back, Sara."

"Hi, Dad." Taylor said brightly as she walked into the living room. "How did everything go with Zoey? Are you getting back together?"

"We're working on it."

"I like Zoey," she said. "Sara's here, Dad."

He smiled. "I told you she'd come around, didn't I."

Taylor bit her bottom lip. "Dad, she's drunk. She's in the bathroom throwing up."

Chapter Four

Hunter sat on the edge of his bed exhausted, but knew that sleep would elude him until he heard Zoey's voice. He'd never believe that Zoey didn't want to see him anymore. He looked at his cell phone. She might not answer if she saw his number. Hunter reached for the burner phone he'd picked up this afternoon. She wouldn't recognize the number and assume it was a business call, and would be sure to answer. He quickly punched in her number. It rang several times before it was picked up.

"Hello," Zoey whispered in a muffled voice.

"Hi, beautiful. I couldn't sleep without telling you that I love you, and forgive you for our unpleasant encounter the other day," he said softly.

"You forgive me? Hunter, I told you that you're not a part of my life anymore. I wish you would get that message through that thick skull of yours! I don't want you to contact me again. Do I make myself clear?" Her voice was cold.

He laughed. "You don't mean it. Admit it. I'm in your blood, and you'll never be able to forget me. And I certainly don't plan to forget you."

"Think what you want. I have no feelings for you," she replied. "Hunter, I'm seeing Daniel again."

He smirked. "Oh, yes, Daniel. The cop who's a million laughs. I recall that you once told me he was only good for passing the time. He bored you to tears."

"I was wrong about him."

He rolled his eyes. "Now don't tell me that he can fulfill your needs better than I."

"For your information, Daniel respects me. Do you hear me, Hunter? Respect. I doubt that word is even in your vocabulary."

"Something must be wrong with him if he can resist your charm. Or is the truth really that he doesn't stimulate your innermost charms?" His voice was low.

"I wouldn't be seeing him again if I didn't have feelings for him."

"I'm the only man who can make you come alive. I light a fire in you that can't be put out. No other man can do that to you. Not even Daniel, no matter how much you want to pretend he can. Do you pretend it's me when you're with him? I'll bet you do. You need me, Zoey. You'll never be free from me."

"Hunter, please stop it," she pleaded. "What do you want from me?"

"You. All I've ever wanted is you."

"I've got to go, Hunter. Don't call me again. Please, for both our sakes."

Hunter chuckled as he set his phone down. He slipped his clothes off, and then slid beneath the cool sheets. He put his hands under his head, staring at the ceiling and felt at peace, with himself and with the world. Hunter was more convinced than ever that Zoey belonged to him. He'd heard her voice trying to hold back her true emotions and knew that her heart was aching for him. He controlled all of her thoughts and emotions, knowing her protests were in vain. She desired him and only him for the rest of her life. Hunter smiled broadly. "Yes, Zoey, my love, you didn't know what you were getting into when you gave your heart to me. We will always be together. Forever," he said aloud.

****

Daniel opened the bathroom door. Sara looked up from her seat on the floor. Her head rested against the side of the toilet bowl.

He walked over to her and firmly, but gently, placed a hand on her shoulder. "Sara, I want to know everything that happened to you tonight."

She tried to lift her head, but nausea overcame her. Daniel grabbed her shoulders, guiding her head back to the bowl. When she was finished vomiting, she sat back down.

"What happened tonight?" he asked again.

She was silent as she wiped her mouth with the cool cloth he handed her. She drew a shuddering breath. "I feel awful."

"How much did you drink?"

"I don't remember."

"Anything stronger than beer?"

"No."

Daniel studied her. "Sara, did you take anything else?"

She squinted up at him. "You mean like drugs?"

"Yes."

"I've never taken any drugs, Mr. Trevors. I never even smoked pot." Her face contorted. "I don't even like alcohol."

Daniel frowned. "Then why do you drink, Sara?"

She swept the hair from her brow. "To fit in. A lot of kids drink. Not Taylor, though."

He nodded. "There are other ways to fit in."

"Not when you come from my family. No one wants to be your friend."

Daniel scratched his chin. "Taylor is your friend. As far as I know she's never judged you, Sara."

"No, she hasn't. I don't know why she wants to be friends with me."

"I'll tell you something. You can blame everyone else for all your problems and continue feeling sorry for yourself, or you can pick yourself up and make something out of your life." His eyes narrowed. "You came here tonight because you know that Taylor is a good friend. But if you continue down this road, trust me, she may not be here for you the next time."

Sara lowered her head.

Daniel hated being tough on her, but he had to reach her. She was a good kid, and he hated to see the road she was headed down. "Sara, now you need to tell me what happened tonight."

Her forehead wrinkled. "I don't know where to start," she said slowly.

He sat on the edge of the bathtub. "Well, the beginning's always a good place."

She sniffed. "I'm seeing Asher Michaels. We went out tonight."

"I've heard of him. He's older than you."

"Yeah. He's my brothers' age...seventeen."

Michaels had had a few minor run-ins with the law. Nothing major, yet, but Daniel knew the boy was headed for trouble. Asher's father was a decent man, but seemed to have little control over his son. As far as the Kane boys were concerned, Daniel assumed they'd eventually end up in prison, as their infractions were growing more serious. Their parents didn't care what happened to them or to Sara. They'd always been allowed to run the streets no matter what time of night. It angered him. The Kanes were alcoholics and lived in a rundown shack. Their children had no family support or guidance and made their own rules. He couldn't remember how many times the police had been to the Kane home to quell a domestic dispute. In the end, though, Mrs. Kane always refused to press charges. Daniel finally concluded that as strange as it appeared, their fighting was what kept them together.

Daniel had been appalled with the deplorable living conditions at the Kane home. The only source of income the family claimed came from the odd jobs Sara's father did until a drinking binge would put him out of work once again. Then the family collected welfare until another job came along. But there was no excuse for the filth. Sara's mother had her own binges, and a clean house or family meals were things the Kane children were not accustomed to. Both parents were guilty of abusing their children through the years, but there was never enough evidence to bring charges against them. It frustrated Daniel to see these kids fall through the cracks.

Even though Sara's home life was abysmal, he saw the potential in her to make something better out of her life. He'd never worried about Taylor being influenced by Sara, and had hoped that some of Taylor's values would rub off on Sara in a positive way. But seeing Sara in this condition caused him concern. He didn't want to forbid Taylor from associating with Sara, but at the same time he worried that possibly, Sara might influence Taylor negatively.

"Did Asher give you the beer?"

She nodded. "Yes. He had some whiskey, too, and wanted me to have some, but I didn't drink any."

"Do you know where he gets the alcohol from?"

"No."

Daniel was thoughtful for a minute. "What happened tonight, Sara?"

She sighed defeated. "This is really hard for me. I told Taylor. Can't she tell you?"

"No, Sara," he said gently. "I need you to tell me. Did Asher hurt you in any way?"

She looked at him and then focused on the wall. "Asher and I always have a few beers together. Well, tonight, like I said, he had some whiskey. He never had whiskey with him before."

"Did he offer you any drugs?"

She shook her head.

"Do you know if he's on drugs?"

"He smokes pot once in a while, but I don't think he's on anything else."

"Okay. What happened?"

"He...he wanted me to...you know...have sex with him. I wouldn't do it." Her face turned a deep shade of red.

"I know this is hard for you, Sara, but I have to ask you these questions," Daniel said. "Did Asher force you to drink with him?"

She emphatically shook her head. "No."

"Did you drink before you met Asher, or did you start when you met him?"

"Sometimes I drank at home. Asher didn't get me started drinking." She looked at her hands that were folded in her lap. "You know how it is, Mr. Trevors. It was always around." She covered her face with her hands. "I only did it to ease the pain. It wouldn't hurt so much then." She sniffed. "Then I could pretend that my family was like everybody else's."

Daniel pitied her. "Sara, what are you leaving out? You know you can trust me."

"I know." She looked into his eyes. "I don't want to get him in trouble." She hesitated.

"Are you talking about Asher?"

She nodded. "Sometimes I think that he's doing more than pot. I think he's on crack or something. He hasn't been acting right lately. He gets mad all the time. He never used to be like that." She twisted her hands together. "My brothers started hanging out with him all the time after they got a new job."

He tried to make sense out of what she was telling him. Her alcohol-induced mind wasn't helping. "Sara, why do you think Asher is taking drugs? And what does that have to do with your brothers' new jobs? Did they hang out with Asher a lot before that?"

"They would talk to Asher when he came to the house, and they worked on their bikes together, but I don't think they hung out anywhere until they started working at their new jobs."

"Do you know who they work for?"

She shook her head. "No, just that they make a lot of money."

Daniel still wasn't connecting the dots. He decided to go back to questioning her about Asher's drug use. "Do you know who is supplying drugs to Asher?"

She swallowed hard. "I don't want to get anybody in trouble." She bit her bottom lip. "Especially since I can't prove it."

"You could be helping Asher, Sara. If he's on something he needs help."

"It's not just him."

Daniel's eyes narrowed. "I thought you said you—"

Sara cut him off. "Not me. I think Randy and Andy have been taking drugs, too. The guy they work for is a real jerk, but they're trying to get Asher a job with him, too, because the pay is really good. They'd never make that kind of money flipping burgers."

"You think they're getting drugs from this man?"

She nodded. "My brothers were fine before they started working for him. Then they started acting angry all the time."

"What do you know about this guy? I thought you didn't know who he was. Do you?"

"No. I don't know his name, but I saw him." Her eyebrows knitted together. "He's weird. I mean, he's not weird looking or anything like that. He dresses really cool, but he's just different."

"How?"

She was thoughtful for a moment. "I don't know." She frowned. "Like he enjoys controlling people. Like he gets off on seeing them squirm."

"You got that just seeing him?"

"It was the way he was walking around Asher, giving him the once over."

"How did Asher react afterwards?"

She bit her bottom lip. "He was pissed, and told me I better not say a word to anybody, especially my brothers."

"Did you think that odd?"

"Not after he explained that there are large amounts of money being picked up. It's for their safety."

Daniel scratched his chin. "Sara, would you recognize this man if you saw him again?"

She cleared her throat. "Yeah, I think I would."

He frowned. "Now this is very important. I want you to think very hard before you answer me." He eyed her carefully.

"Okay."

"Why do you think this man is supplying drugs to your brothers?"

She shrugged. "I don't know...just the way they act since they started working for him."

"Do you know this man's name?"

"I already told you no." She drew a deep breath. "Why do you keep asking me the same questions over and over?"

Daniel studied her. "Because you've had quite a bit to drink tonight, and I need to know that you understand my questions. Would you rather answer them tomorrow when you're feeling better?"

"No. I don't think I'll feel better for a long time."

His eyes drifted to her wrists. "What happened, Sara? How did you get those marks on your wrists?"

Her face flushed. "It was an accident."

"It wasn't an accident, Sara," Daniel said firmly. "Did Asher do that to you?"

"He's never done anything like that before. He would never hurt me deliberately."

"Are you telling me the truth when you said he didn't sexually assault you?"

"Yes."

Daniel rubbed his chin. "Okay, let's get back to your brothers' boss. Have you ever heard them mention his name?"

"No. They only call him Mr. D. They meet him at a huge abandoned building."

Daniel's interest piqued. "Is that where they work?"

"No. They just meet him there and he sends them to their jobs."

"Do you remember where the building is located, Sara?"

She rubbed her forehead. "Yeah. It's on the east side. It's kind of rural."

Something clicked in his brain. The abandoned warehouse was where Stephanie Rinehart said her brother had met a man he was running drugs for. This couldn't be a coincidence. "Do you know what their jobs are, Sara?" He hoped this could give him the first solid link to finding the serial killer.

"I think it's some sort of delivery service. I don't know."

"How did you meet Mr. D?"

"I didn't. One night I drove out there with Asher. My brothers set up an interview for him with the guy. I waited outside on Asher's bike. Asher told me he had to meet him alone, and I should stay back where he parked the bike. I don't know why he parked a ways from the building. It was creepy out there with nothing around. I was scared. I could see a light from the building so I walked closer to wait for Asher. I made sure Mr. D couldn't see me, but I could see him in the doorway."

Daniel listened patiently as Sara slurred and stumbled over her words. He was surprised that she was talking at all and hadn't passed out by now. He wrung out the cloth and handed it back to Sara. "Do you think you'd recognize him again?"

"Yeah…maybe. Especially his glasses and mustache."

Daniel's adrenalin started pumping. Mr. D sounded like the same man Stephanie Rinehart described. "Sara, I'm going to ask a very important favor of you."

She nodded.

"Everything you told me tonight I want you to keep just between us. I don't want you to tell your brothers or Asher that you told me anything about their jobs or Mr. D. Okay?"

"Is something wrong?" Her eyes widened. "They're not in trouble, are they?"

"I hope not, but I need your word on this."

"Okay, I won't tell them."

"Are you feeling better?"

"Yeah, better than I thought I would. The last time…." Her voice trailed off and her face flushed.

Daniel wanted to lecture her, but would wait until morning. She looked exhausted. He'd go over everything she told him tonight when her mind was clearer. He patted her shoulder. "We'll talk more in the morning."

She nodded. "Mr. Trevors, would it be okay if I stayed here tonight?"

He smiled. "Of course. I'll give your parents a call."

Her face darkened. "Don't bother. They won't know whether I'm home or not."

****

Andrew and Randall Kane had been inseparable since their births seventeen years earlier. They loved their younger sister Sara, looked out for her, and tried to protect her. The three of them had grown up enjoying a closeness with one another that many siblings didn't share. They'd had to parent themselves and one another. Even though they had their fair share of arguments and disagreements, they remained close. When Sara started bringing Asher Michaels around, Randy and Andy kept a closer watch on her, but Asher seemed okay. They liked Asher and grew fond of him. Eventually, he began coming over to see them as much as their sister. The brothers made it perfectly clear to Asher what would happen if he ever violated their sister in any way.

Asher knew everything there was to know about motorcycles, and the three young men were often found working together on their bikes. When Asher learned how much money Randy and Andy were making in their new jobs, he wanted in. He knew he could never make that much money sweating his life away at some gas station. He and the Kane boys had occasionally dabbled in drugs, but preferred pot.

Andy Kane tapped on Asher Michaels' apartment door. While he waited, he looked up and down the street. A few boys

72

were playing ball in the road, and a couple of women were seated on a stoop next door holding coffee mugs in their hands while their children played nearby.

He glanced at his wristwatch. "Dammit," he muttered under his breath. He pounded on the door with his fist, which caused the women to halt their conversation and eye him suspiciously.

"Yeah, coming!" a muffled voice called from inside. A moment later Asher stood half-dressed in the doorway.

"What are you doing? We're going to be late!" Andy said impatiently. "I told you to be ready."

Asher yawned. "Sorry. I fell asleep, and when I woke up, I grabbed a shower."

"Well, come on. We've got to go. I hope we're not late."

"Hold on a minute. Let me at least put my boots on." He grabbed a T-shirt, then pulled his boots on. He hurried out of the apartment, slamming the door shut behind him. Andy was already on his bike, revving the engine. A couple of minutes later, Asher slid on the seat behind him.

Twenty minutes after that, they pulled up in front of the Morgan Hotel. They slid off the bike, walked to the front door, and peered inside.

"What next?" Asher asked.

"I don't know. Mr. D said to wait here for the pickup."

"Where's Randy?"

"He had another delivery on the East Side."

"Oh." He stuffed his hands into his jeans' pockets. "So, did Mr. D make up his mind if I'm in or not?" he finally asked, raising an eyebrow.

Andy shrugged. "He didn't say. You never know what he's thinking or planning to do. He acts like he's your best friend one minute, and cold as hell the next." He shook his head. "He's strange, never gives you a straight answer about anything. If you ask too many questions he goes off. I guess he'll contact you if you're in." His eyes narrowed. "If you're not, though, let me give you a word of warning. Forget you ever met him. Don't mention his name to a soul."

"Why?" Asher asked.

"Just don't. I heard a guy got beaten pretty badly for opening his mouth." He exhaled loudly. "Mr. D has connections in high places, and nothing will ever lead back to him."

"I'll keep that in mind." Asher scratched his jaw. "Has Sara said anything about me?" He nervously shuffled his feet. "I really miss her."

"Nah. You know girls. She's just playing hard to get." He eyed him. "Must have been one hell of a fight. Guess you'll have to send flowers," he chuckled.

Asher wondered why Sara hadn't told her brothers what he'd done. But he was glad she hadn't. He put his hand on his brow, shielding his eyes from the bright sun as he glanced up the street. He nudged Andy. "Do you think this is him?"

Andy frowned. "Hard to tell."

They watched a man confidently making his way toward them. He was mid-thirties, average looks and height, and professionally dressed, looking like a banker or lawyer.

"I bet he doesn't get his clothes at the thrift store." Asher laughed.

Andy smiled. "Doesn't look like it."

The man stopped in front of them and gave them a swift once over. "Kane?" he asked in a deep voice.

"Yes," Andy replied.

"Who are you?" He looked disapprovingly at Asher. "I wasn't informed there would be two of you."

"He's with me," Andy said quickly. "He's waiting for Mr. D's approval to begin working. I'm just showing him the ropes."

"Does Mr. D know this?" His eyebrows knitted together.

Andy swallowed hard. "One of us always brings the new guy with us a couple of times."

"But you stated he's waiting for approval. He hasn't been hired yet."

Andy's face reddened.

"Never mind. I'll deal with that later," the man said impatiently as he swiftly scanned the street. "Come with me. There's a coffee shop a couple of doors down."

They followed him into the coffee shop, where he led them to a secluded table in the back of the room. He ordered three cups of coffee, and then turned to Andy. "You have something for me?"

"Yes." Andy started to reach into his jacket pocket, but the man grabbed his wrist.

"It's obvious that you're new, too."

Andy looked questionably at him. "Not too new."

"Then you haven't been properly trained yourself." His voice was cold. "Slowly take the envelope out of your pocket and lay it on the table." He watched the waitress nearing their table. He kept his grip on Andy's wrist. "Wait until she serves the coffee." He let go of the boy's wrist.

They sat in silence until she returned with their beverages. "May I get you anything else?" the waitress asked.

"No, thank you," he answered with a polite smile.

Andy watched as she walked to another table, then following the man's instructions, slowly reached into his pocket and withdrew the envelope. He kept it in the palm of his hand, and then rested his hand on the table. He waited for the man to make the next move.

The man glanced down at the envelope, then quickly slid it off the table and peeked inside. "Everything seems to be in order," he said as he took an envelope from his breast pocket and slipped it under Andy's coffee saucer. "I deducted a couple of hundred because I was ripped off the last time."

"Wait a minute," Andy protested. "I'm not supposed to give you anything unless the money's all here."

"That's your problem, not mine," the man answered, abruptly standing up. He threw a few bills on the table, and then quickly walked away.

"This is just great," Andy muttered. "I don't know what I'm going to do now." He ran his hand through his hair.

"I'll go with you when you meet Mr. D. At least I can be a witness," Asher offered.

"No, I'd better go alone. Besides, I didn't exactly have the okay to bring you along today." He shrugged. "What can he do but fire me?"

Asher smiled as he slapped his friend on the back. "Easy come, easy go."

"Yeah, the money was good while it lasted." His eyes narrowed. "Let's get out of here." He stood up. "Want a lift back home?"

"No. I think I'll hang around down here for a while. Come over tomorrow and let me know how you made out. Good luck, Andy."

"Yeah, I'm going to need a lot of luck about now."

****

Andy pulled up to the warehouse, got off his motorcycle, and then cautiously walked inside the building. "I'm here!" he called. He looked around the dirty building, and then glanced at his wristwatch. It wasn't like Mr. D to be late for a pick up.

He didn't know what to do. He put his hands into his pockets, nervously fingering the envelope.

"I see you made it, Kane."

The voice startled him. He turned around to face the man. "Yeah, I've been here for a few minutes," he said as he pulled the envelope from his pocket. "I got the money here." He nervously cleared his throat. "But there's a slight problem." He thrust the envelope at him.

"I don't like problems," Mr. D replied, taking the envelope.

Andy felt perspiration running down his back as he stared into the man's cold steely eyes. "He said he didn't get all his stuff the last time so he deducted a couple hundred. I don't know if he did or not since the envelopes are always sealed."

Mr. D exhaled loudly. He opened the envelope and slowly counted the money. "I don't make mistakes, and I don't tolerate mistakes from my employees." His voice was icy. "How long have you been working for me, Kane?"

"A couple of months, I guess."

"Have I ever withheld any of your pay?"

"No."

"So why are you holding out on me?"

"I'm...I'm not," Andy stuttered. "I swear."

He fingered the money, slowly counting it again. "There's five hundred missing."

"He told me two hundred." Andy's eyes darted back and forth. "He ripped you off, not me!"

Mr. D firmly placed a hand on Andy's shoulder. "Five hundred dollars is a lot of money. Wouldn't you say so? A young man could do a lot of things with that much money." His voice was flat. "How do I know that you didn't take it? You can't prove it, now can you?" He didn't give Andy a chance to reply. "Do you think you can pull a fast one on me?" He kept his eyes focused on Andy as he reached into his pocket.

Andy trembled with fear as perspiration soaked his body. He noted the wire-rimmed glasses Mr. D wore. Could he knock the glasses off him? Maybe he couldn't see without his glasses. Then he could make a run for it. At least it might buy him some time.

Before Andy could make his move, the man grabbed him firmly, and then pointed a glistening knife at him, holding it so the point was against the boy's throat. "I don't like to be double crossed."

"I didn't do anything!" Andy cried in fear. "I didn't steal your money, but I'll pay you back every cent you think I took!" he choked. One move and the knife would be plunged into his throat. He had to think fast, but his mind was frozen in fear.

The man shook his head. "You know what doesn't make sense? Why would you be willing to pay back money you insist you didn't take?" His forehead furrowed. "Sounds like that's an admission."

"I...I don't know, but you've got to believe me when I tell you that I didn't touch the money. The envelope was sealed...you saw it! They're always sealed."

Mr. D laughed. "If you would have counted it like you were instructed, it wouldn't have been sealed, now would it?"

"I didn't touch it because you told us to never open an envelope if it's sealed. Every envelope I've delivered and picked up has been sealed. You never said anything before," Andy protested.

"Are you calling me a liar?"

"No."

"Now where would you get the money to pay me back?"

"I don't know." His eyes pleaded with Mr. D's for mercy.

"Maybe you could deduct it from my pay."

The man frowned. "Maybe I could," he said slowly, "but I'm not going to." He grinned as he playfully poked the knife between Andy's ribs. "Maybe there's another way."

Andy suddenly realized what Mr. D was planning to do. "You're going to kill me!"

The man continued grinning, watching him plead for his life. He was enjoying himself and seemed pumped up with the power to determine whether Andy lived or died. Andy's heart pounded.

****

Daniel finished his drink and rose. "I'd better be going."

"Do you have to, Daniel?" Zoey asked. "I was hoping we could talk for a little while."

He nodded. "I suppose a little longer won't hurt."

"Good. Why don't you sit back down and I'll get you another drink?"

He held up a hand. "I don't care for another drink. I need to keep a clear head." He sat back down on the sofa.

She cocked an eye. "Because of me?"

He laughed. "No."

"You had me scared for a minute there. I take it you can't spend the night."

"No, I don't want to leave Taylor alone."

"Maybe I could stay at your place?"

"You know how I feel about that." He'd love nothing more than to wake up next to her, but he didn't want to send the wrong message to his daughter. She wasn't naïve, and he was certain she knew Zoey and he had slept together, but he didn't feel right doing it in his home with her there.

"I know and I respect that," Zoey replied. "But we could change that."

Daniel exhaled. "We both need time."

Zoey sat next to him. "Daniel, I was wrong. I see that now. I was afraid I wouldn't measure up."

"Are my standards that high?" he asked. "You never mentioned that before."

"It was a lot of things. There was also Taylor to consider."

"You and Taylor have always gotten along," Daniel reasoned. "She's crazy about you."

"I was afraid that would change."

Daniel listened, but a part of him still wasn't convinced. There was more, but for whatever reason, she wouldn't or couldn't tell him what had changed her mind then and why she was pushing it now.

"Now we can take our time and work through whatever it was that you were worried about before." He saw a dark shadow pass over her face. "Let's just enjoy what we have now." He drew her to him. "I don't have to leave this very minute." He ran a hand up her skirt.

She pressed herself close to him and he felt her breath quicken as he began to kiss her deeply.

CHAPTER FIVE

A group of girls chatted and enjoyed the sunny warm weather as they slowly walked down the street headed to their weekly Saturday morning dance class at the Davis Dance Studio two doors down. Something glittering in an alleyway caught one of the teen's attention. She abruptly stopped and squinted at the object.

"What's up, Meg?" one of the teens asked.

Meg pointed at a glistening object. "I wonder what it is. I'm going to check it out."

"Who cares?" a girl named Becca asked. "It's probably a can or something."

"It could be something valuable. You never know. I'm going to find out," Meg stated.

"I doubt it. Come on. We'll be late for class," Becca warned.

Meg frowned. "It'll only take a minute. Maybe it's a ring or necklace. Ms. Davis won't care if we're a few minutes late."

Becca looked at the other girls. "Go ahead if you want, but I think I'll go with Meg to check it out."

The rest of the girls slowly made their way down the alley

following Meg and Becca. When they reached the object, which glistened under the bright sun, they looked at the ground, and then halted, frozen in their tracks. After a few seconds they looked at one another, and then ran screaming in terror down the alley and tore breathlessly into the dance studio.

"Ms. Davis! Ms. Davis!" Meg panted.

Zoey hurried over to Meg. She placed her hands on the girl's shoulders. "Calm down, Meg. You girls look like you've seen a ghost." She scrutinized each of them. They were pale and trembling. "Will someone please calmly tell me what's happened?"

"In the alley," Becca stuttered. "There's a guy! He's dead."

Zoey lifted an eyebrow. "Becca, it's probably a homeless person. I'm sure he's just sleeping."

"No," Meg said. "He's not moving." She drew a shuddering breath. "There's blood all over!"

****

Daniel Trevors and Ben Wilson stood peering down at the body.

"I wonder who it is," Ben said. "Any ID on him?"

"Yeah." Daniel sucked in his breath as he opened the wallet and looked at the driver's license. "It's Andy Kane," he answered. He squatted and examined the puncture wounds. The jacket was shredded on one side. "Damn," he muttered as Sara and his conversation popped into his mind. "Ben, remember Stephanie Rinehart's description of the guy she saw at the warehouse with her brother?"

"Yeah, why?"

"A couple of nights ago Sara Kane, who happens to be Taylor's best friend, described the same guy. She said he had a mustache and wore wire-rimmed glasses, and gave the same

82

description of the way he was dressed."

"It can't be a coincidence."

"That's what I was thinking." He paused. "She also mentioned the warehouse. We need to check it out."

"I agree. What doesn't make sense to me, though, is why he would use an abandoned building to do his dealings. If he owned the building I could see, but using someone else's property is a big risk."

Daniel frowned. "Maybe he gets off on that. Sara said he goes by the name Mr. D."

Ben's eyes shifted. "That's not much to go on."

"No, but it's more than we had." Daniel looked again at the corpse.

"Will the girl cooperate with us?" Ben asked.

Daniel sighed. "I think she will, but it's going to be rough."

"Why?"

Daniel looked Ben in the eye. "I told you…she's our latest victim's sister. I dread breaking the news to the family."

"Are you close to them?" Ben asked. "I know we've had a few calls to the Kane's."

"No, nothing like that. I know Sara only because of her friendship with Taylor. She's at our house often. She's a good kid, Ben."

"I'm sure she is. I would think because it's her brother that would make her more inclined to help in any way she can to catch his killer."

Daniel shook his head. "We've got a serial killer on our hands and he's not going to stop." He looked down the alley. "It could be anybody."

"Did Sara say anything else? Was her brother running drugs like Stephanie Rinehart's?"

"She doesn't know. She said Andy and his twin brother Randy made deliveries. Her brothers took the job because of the money." His eyebrows drew together. "Their friend Asher Michaels was hoping to get a job with Mr. D, too."

"This isn't just about a drug ring. Mr. D lures them in with the sole intention of murdering them." Ben looked at Daniel. "We've got to find him before he strikes again."

"And we've got to talk to Randy Kane and Asher Michaels. They could be his next victims."

****

Ben and Daniel pulled up in front of the Kane's ramshackle house. They got out of the car and made their way up the crumbling sidewalk to the front door.

A form appeared briefly in the dirty window and then the door was flung open, revealing a woman, about mid-forties, who was clothed in a filthy housecoat, which hung loosely on her underweight frame.

"What is it this time?" she snarled at the detectives. "I know that Andy must be in some kind of trouble again since he didn't come home last night."

"May we come in, Mrs. Kane?" Daniel asked.

"I suppose." She led them to the sofa, scooting off two cats that had been napping together on one end. The cats lazily made their way to a table at the end of the room, curling up underneath and resuming their naps. "Have a seat."

Ben looked at Daniel, raising his eyes as she moved a stack of newspapers and magazines from the middle of the sofa. "We're fine," he told her.

"Could you please get the rest of the family?" Daniel asked the woman.

Mrs. Kane placed her hands on her hips. "Look, Bill's in bed.

He was sick last night, so if it's not too important, I don't want to wake him." She looked around the room. "Besides, I've got a lot of housework to get to."

"This is important, Mrs. Kane," he insisted. "Please get him."

She grunted and then huffed out of the room.

"This place should be condemned," Ben muttered under his breath, eyeing the collection of empty beer cans and whiskey bottles littering the coffee table and floor.

"I feel sorry for the kids," Daniel said.

"I know what you mean. How can people live like this?"

Loud angry voices drifted in from another part of the house. A few minutes later, Bill Kane sauntered into the room. His dingy gray T-shirt barely covered his sagging stomach. He hiked up his jogging pants. Daniel wondered if it was to cover his bulging stomach or to try to hide the gaping hole in his T-shirt. He kicked a couple of beer cans out of his way. His wife trailed him.

"So what brings you here this time?" he asked, staring bleary eyed at them. "If Andy's got himself in another mess, then he can just sit and rot in jail for all I care. That boy is nothing but trouble!" He turned as his daughter entered the room. "I've got things to do." He turned to leave.

"Please wait, Mr. Kane," Ben said quietly.

"Make it quick."

Sara seated herself in an overstuffed chair and looked at the detectives. Bill Kane walked behind the chair in which Sara sat, suspiciously eyeing the men. Mary Kane walked next to her husband and grabbed his arm.

"This is bad news, isn't it?" Mrs. Kane's voice slightly trembled. "I've got a bad feeling. If it wasn't bad you wouldn't want us all here."

Daniel cleared his throat. "Mr. and Mrs. Kane, and Sara,

I'm sorry, but we do have some bad news." He looked at Sara and saw her stiffen. Her eyes were fearful. He hated being the bearer of this news, but it had to be done. Delaying the inevitable wouldn't change the fact that Andrew Kane was dead. "We found Andrew's body in the alley on Fourth Street this morning. His wallet with his driver's license was found on him, but we still need one of you to make a positive identification of the body." He looked at the family. Their faces were grief stricken. "I'm sorry for your loss," he said, even though he knew his words offered cold comfort no matter how sorry he really was.

Sara screamed. "No! It can't be Andy! Please, Mr. Trevors. Maybe it's somebody else. Maybe somebody robbed him and took his wallet."

Mary and Bill Kane stared at each other in disbelief. "What happened? How did he die?" Bill finally asked, lighting a cigarette with a shaky hand.

"He was murdered," Ben answered gently.

Sara's hand flew to her mouth. "Oh my God!" she moaned.

Daniel turned to her. "Sara, we need your help."

"How can she help?" Bill Kane asked. "What has she got to do with this?"

"Mr. Kane, do you know who your son worked for?" Ben asked, changing the conversation.

"No, he was always picking up odd jobs. We had a strained relationship." He eyed the detectives. "It doesn't mean I didn't care about my boy." He turned his attention back to Daniel. "You still haven't answered my question. How can Sara help?"

"She may be able to identify the man responsible."

"Now wait a minute," Bill Kane said. "Isn't that putting her life at risk?"

"She saw a man who we believe hired your son to run drugs.

We would like Sara to describe this man to a sketch artist in order to do a composite. Now if she could come down to the station with us—"

"No! You have no right to ask us to risk our daughter's life!" he interrupted. He ran a shaky hand through his hair. "We haven't even had time to digest this news."

"Mr. Kane, there would be no risk to your daughter. She may be the only one who can identify his killer," Ben explained.

"No." He swallowed hard. "Not today or ever," he said. "What if this murderer finds out that Sara identified him? I've already lost one child, and I'll be damned if I'll lose another."

Sara jumped up, wiping the tears from her eyes. "What right do you have to act so concerned with my life when you never gave a damn about me, Dad? And you never cared about Andy or Randy! All you care about is your booze!"

"That's enough, Sara!" Mary said sharply. "Show some respect for your father!"

She laughed. "That's a good one, Mom. Your son, my brother, has just been murdered! Has it sunk in? Look at this pigsty you call our home! Neither one of you has cared about any of us!"

Bill Kane walked over to her. "A girl should treat her father with respect."

Daniel watched as Sara's eyes filled with tears. "Maybe I would, Dad, if you acted like a father. All you care about is yourself." She wiped at her eyes. "Why did you and Mom ever have kids? You shouldn't have had kids." Her voice broke. "Maybe if you had cared about us even a little, Andy would still be alive!"

Bill Kane mopped his forehead with the back of his hand. "I never meant to hurt my family." He looked at his daughter. "You're right, Sara. I never should have fathered children. I can't even take care of myself, so how could I expect to take care of a family?" His eyes brimmed with tears. "It hasn't totally hit me yet about Andy, but I swear it will, and you don't know what his death will do to me. He was my son, my flesh and blood." He placed a hand on Sara's shoulder. "You're right, Sara. You need to do whatever you can to help the police." He put an arm around his wife's shoulder. She was sobbing uncontrollably. He drew her close to him. "Mary, I think it's high time you and I took a long hard look at ourselves and what we've done to our lives and our children's lives. We have nothing to show for ourselves. We need help, Mary. It won't bring our boy back to us, but maybe we can make things better for Randy and Sara. We have to try."

Mary Kane gripped his arm as tears flowed freely from her eyes. "I'll do whatever it takes, Bill. I only know that we have to stop the pain."

Daniel knew the grief on their faces was genuine. "I can send someone over to make arrangements for treatment for the both of you at the local alcohol abuse center after your son's burial if you'd like."

Bill Kane grabbed Daniel's hand. "Thank you, Detective Trevors."

"Temporary foster care can also be arranged for Sara, but I would be happy to have her stay with Taylor and me," he offered.

Sara looked hopefully at her father. "Please, Dad?"

He nodded. "That would be best."

"Sara, I know that this is a difficult time for you, but do you think you could come down to the station with us now?"

"Yes, Mr. Trevors, I want to help in any way I can."

****

Daniel handed Sara a can of soda. "Don't be nervous, Sara." He introduced her to the sketch artist. "I'll be back later. If you need or want anything, don't be afraid to ask."

She nodded. "Okay."

Daniel walked over to his desk and checked his messages. "Ready to go talk to Asher Michaels?" he asked Ben, who was leafing through a folder.

Ben glanced up at him. "Yeah." He closed the folder. "We should have asked Stephanie Rinehart to do a composite, too."

"She didn't get as good of a look at him as Sara did. But if this doesn't pan out, we can get her down here to do one and compare them. Maybe one of them will pick up on something the other missed."

"Sounds like a plan. Who's driving?"

"You are." Daniel threw him the keys.

They walked to the car and Daniel slid into the passenger seat. He checked his cell phone messages while Ben started the car.

"How's it going with Zoey?"

"Slow. At least on my part."

Ben cocked an eyebrow as he pulled into traffic. "Sounds like things have reversed this time around."

"Yeah. I still care about her as much as I did before, but I'm not ready to just pick up where we left off like nothing ever happened. She's never given me a clear reason for breaking off."

"You don't trust her?"

"I don't know. I want to, but something is nagging in the back of my mind."

"Maybe she had cold feet. You know you were talking marriage. She wasn't ready then, but is now."

"Well, this time around her feet seemed to have warmed up quite a bit. And very fast."

"And that makes you suspicious?" He chuckled. "Why don't

you just relax and enjoy the ride? Unless you think she's hiding some deep dark secret." Ben screwed up his face. "I got it…she's our serial killer! Hiding right under your nose."

Daniel laughed. "Okay, okay, I get your message. I need to enjoy what I have. You're right."

"I am," he grinned. "As usual."

Daniel leaned back in the seat. "So, what's got you in such a good mood today?" he asked.

Ben glanced at him. "I might be able to have Josh with me for the entire summer. Not just a couple of weeks."

"That's great news. How did you swing it with Clare?"

"I sweet talked her." He grinned.

Daniel laughed. "Sure you did. Really, Ben, it seems like an abrupt reversal. What changed her mind?"

Ben gripped the steering wheel. "Let's just say she got her pound of flesh."

Daniel wanted to press him for details, but by the hardened expression on his partner's face, he let it drop. They rode in silence for a few minutes.

"This looks like the place," Ben announced as they pulled up in front of a building. A young man was tinkering with a motorcycle parked on the sidewalk leading to the building.

"You think that's him?" Daniel asked.

"There's only one way to find out," Ben replied.

They got out of the car and walked to where the man was squatted next to his bike, a tool chest at his side. He looked up as they approached, set down the wrench, wiped his hands on an oily rag, then stood facing them.

"Are you Asher Michaels?" Daniel asked.

He looked at them suspiciously. "Who wants to know?"

"We do," Ben answered as he and Daniel flashed their ID's.

"I didn't do anything." Asher's eyes slanted as he scowled at them.

"No one said you did. That's not why we're here," Ben said. "We need to ask you a few questions."

"Look, I'm kind of busy."

"Really?" Ben asked. "Working on your bike?"

"Yeah, I need it for work."

Daniel caught Asher's eye. "Where do you work?"

Asher shuffled his feet. "I'm looking for a job. I might have one."

Ben walked around the bike examining it. "I thought you said you need your bike for work."

"I do." He rammed his hands into his pockets.

"Do you have a job right now?" Ben asked.

"Not exactly…I'll know soon. That's what I meant. I need my bike if I get the job." He moved closer to his bike. "Am I in some kind of trouble?"

"No," Daniel said. "We'd like to ask you a few questions."

"What about?"

"The job you might get."

Asher's eyebrows squinted together. "How can I answer questions when I don't have the job yet?"

"Do you know a Mr. D?" Ben asked abruptly.

The color drained from Asher's face. He sucked in his breath. "Who told you about him?"

"That doesn't matter," Ben said. "Do you know him?"

Asher looked nervously around the nearly deserted street. "I gotta go. I'm not answering any of your questions."

"Are you afraid of him, Asher?" Daniel asked.

"Look, I never said I know him."

Daniel noticed how Asher's eyes shifted. He knew him and

he was scared shitless, but he was tightlipped. "When was the last time you saw Andy and Randy Kane?"

His brow furrowed. "I don't know. Maybe a day or two." He eyed Daniel warily. "Look, if they got in trouble, it has nothing to do with me."

"No one said they were in trouble," Daniel said. So, Asher didn't know that one of his best friends had been murdered. He looked at Ben.

"Did you see Andy or Randy Kane yesterday?"

Without answering Asher hopped on his bike, and seconds later roared down the street. Daniel and Ben stood staring after him.

"Well, that was interesting," Ben said.

"We've got to find this Mr. D.," Daniel said. "Sara was right when she told me he seems to have some kind of control over his runners."

"Yeah, it's called fear," Ben stated.

CHAPTER SIX

Bella drew a bath and then walked into the adjoining bedroom and picked up her cell phone. She called Zoey's number.

"Hello," Zoey answered.

"Hi, I just wanted to remind you about our dinner plans tonight."

"Oh, Bella, I'm so sorry. I've completely forgotten about it."

"Zoey! Don't tell me that. You didn't ask Daniel?"

"Sorry. It's been one of those weeks. I'll call him right now and see if he can make it."

"Even if he can't, I still want you to come. But I was hoping that Hunter and Ben could become better acquainted. With Daniel's crazy hours and Hunter going out of town so often for business, they've barely had a chance to sit down and talk."

"I know. I promise to give Daniel a call and let you know."

"I'll expect you to be here at seven with or without Daniel," Bella said.

Bella set her phone down, and then picked up a framed photo from the night side table. She smiled at the picture of Hunter. Just looking at him made her heartbeat quicken. She touched her

93

diamond. Her life was complete…well, almost. Once they were married, everything she ever wanted would be hers.

****

Zoey studied her body in the mirror. She patted her stomach and frowned. Last month she'd missed a period, but attributed it to nerves. But when she had missed one this month, she knew that something was wrong. This morning she'd taken a pregnancy test and nervously read the results. Her worst fears were confirmed. She was carrying Hunter's baby. She considered passing it off as Daniel's, even though she'd become pregnant before they got back together. He would be a wonderful father. He'd already proved it with the way he was raising Taylor. She frowned. He wasn't rushing back into the relationship like she thought he would. They were sleeping together again, but he wasn't the same man he'd been before she'd abruptly broken up with him. Marriage and total commitment were two things he avoided talking about. Now he was cautious, and she couldn't blame him. Even if she could trick him into believing the baby was his and convince him to marry her for the baby's sake, she couldn't deceive him. Eventually he would do the math and figure out that the baby didn't belong to him. He might even demand a DNA test. She took a deep breath and slowly let it out. Maybe she would get an abortion. Or maybe she would keep the baby and raise it alone. She didn't know what to do.

She needed to talk to Hunter. After all, it was his child, too. He'd be a poor excuse for a father, but she was damned if she was going to go through this alone. He would probably become angry, and that frightened her. And he most likely would deny that he was the father. She could threaten him with a paternity test. She chewed her bottom lip. Maybe she should just go somewhere and be done with it. No one would ever know. Neither Daniel nor Hunter would find out, and she could resume the normal life she craved with Daniel. She had a lot of soul searching to do. Normally Bella was the one she ran to, to help her sort out her problems, but now she was on her own.

The guilt of what she'd done to Bella was eating her alive. She couldn't stand being in the same room with her when Hunter was around, but it didn't seem to bother him one bit. That disgusted her. For all she knew Bella and she may not even be the only women in his life. He was a player, and he had played the both of them. Bella was looking forward to a beautiful future with the man she loved, but Zoey knew that Bella's life would be filled with nothing but heartbreak. Without his looks, Hunter Tucker was nothing but a shallow, cold human being…and sometimes she wondered if he was even human. Ice ran through his veins. He had no heart or conscience. He was worse than a narcissist if that was possible. He was a vile human being. But he had an animal magnetism that made even the most sensible woman succumb to him as though she had no control.

She squeezed her eyes shut. Daniel was everything Hunter was not. Just thinking about Daniel brought a smile to her lips. He was the kindest and most gentle man she'd ever met. Why had it taken her so long to realize that he was the man she had truly loved all along? They'd had an instant connection on their first meeting, which over time had grown to a full-blown love affair that Daniel had wanted to take further. But then Hunter had entered the picture and she'd thrown everything away. She ran her hand through her hair. This was doing her no good, rehashing over and over what she'd done. She couldn't change it and she couldn't keep it buried inside. She had to come clean, and the sooner the better. Bella had a right to know the truth about the man she was taking for her husband. If she still wanted to go through with the wedding, then at least Zoey would know she'd warned her. She drew a deep breath. She was terrified to tell Bella, but she had to.

Daniel was her rock...well he had been, and she missed the closeness they'd once shared. He was holding back, and no matter what she did or said to try to convince him that she wanted more, he wouldn't budge. But it didn't matter now. Once he found out the truth, he'd run as fast and as far as he could from her. Zoey couldn't blame him. She didn't deserve him, and she doubted they would ever again share what they'd once had. She'd broken his heart once, but after he learned the truth about her and Hunter, it would be over for good with no chance of reconciliation, ever. Her heart squeezed. Zoey had no one to blame but herself, and now it was time to face the consequences. She toyed once again with the idea of not telling Daniel or Bella. She lifted an eyebrow. Maybe she wouldn't even have to tell Hunter about the baby. Could she hatch a plan to pass it off as Daniel's? Biting down on her bottom lip, she calculated how far along she was and when she and Daniel had started sleeping together again. No, it wouldn't work. She'd have to say the baby was early and it would come too early to be believable. If she told Daniel she was pregnant, he would definitely marry her...that was just the type of man he was. But the truth would eventually come out once she had the baby. He would still end up leaving her.

Maybe she should just pack up and leave the city. She'd cut all ties and just disappear. She'd go somewhere far away and raise her child on her own. Zoey was mentally and emotionally exhausted. As she sat and contemplated her situation, her face suddenly brightened. She was assuming that the two people she cherished most in the world would desert her, but it wasn't fact and she wouldn't know unless she confessed to them. Could they possibly find it in their hearts to forgive her? Was it too much to hope for? Maybe they would understand. If Daniel could somehow find it in his heart to forgive her, she vowed to do everything in her power to make it up to him, even if it took the rest of her life. She needed and wanted him.

She dreaded the dinner with Hunter and Bella tonight, but there was no way to avoid it. She promised Bella she would be there with or without Daniel.

****

Daniel grabbed the phone. "Detective Trevors."

"Hi, Daniel, I'm sorry to bother you at work, but I forgot about a dinner engagement tonight that we were invited to. It's with Bella and Hunter. Can you make it? I'm sorry it's such short notice."

He rubbed his jaw as he leaned back in his chair. "I'm sorry, Zoey, but I can't make it. I'm swamped with work, and I don't even know what time I'll get out of here."

"Maybe we can get together tomorrow night?"

"I can't make any promises right now." He paused. "I'll let you know." He looked at the composite Ben laid on his desk. The man looked vaguely familiar to him. "I've got to go. I'll try to call you later, but I may be here half the night." He hung up and then picked up the composite and studied it.

"You recognize him?" Ben asked.

Daniel frowned. "I've seen this guy before, but I can't place him." He looked at Sara. "Are you sure you never heard him called by any other name?"

She shook her head as she placed the hot dog she had been nibbling on back into its paper holder.

"Somebody's got to know who this guy is." Daniel stared at the sketch before handing it back to Ben.

"I'll run a match," Ben said.

Daniel turned his attention back to Sara. "Sara, is there anything else you can tell me about this guy?" he prodded. "Think. Any little thing you remember about him? You're sure you didn't see a tattoo or scar?"

She sipped her soda and then set the can on the desk. "I've told you everything I can think of, Mr. Trevors." She bit her bottom lip. "I wasn't close enough to see if he had a scar or tattoo."

He nodded. "Okay. I think we're done here now. I'll run you home."

She swallowed hard and then picked her can of soda back up. "I don't want to go home. Can I stay at your house?"

Daniel was surprised. "Don't you want to be with your parents and Randy?"

"I do and I don't." She shook her head. "I know my parents said they're going to get help, but with Andy's death, I don't think they can start right away." Her lips trembled and tears filled her eyes. "I can't fault them for that, but I just can't deal with it right now. They'll be drinking more than ever even if they said they won't." She swiped at her eyes. "I'll tell them I don't want to wait till they go to rehab to stay at your house. Randy will understand, and he'll probably be relieved that I have somewhere to go."

Daniel laid a fatherly hand on her shoulder. "I understand, and of course you can stay. We'll stop by your house so you can pack a few things and find out about your brother's funeral arrangements."

"I still can't believe he's dead." She shuddered. "Life is weird." Tears formed in her eyes. "He was only seventeen. Just because he quit school didn't mean he was stupid. The other night he was telling me about his plans for the future. I really believed that he would be something someday. He was really smart." She looked at Daniel for affirmation. "Especially with fixing cars and motorcycles."

"I'm sure he was," he said softly.

"He could really play the guitar." She smiled. "He used to make up these dumb songs. Especially when I was down. He always said that no matter how bad you felt now, tomorrow would be brighter. He was so optimistic. I don't know what Randy will do without him. I think they would have been close even if they weren't twins. They did everything together; even getting the same jobs." The realization of what she had just said suddenly filled her with fear. "Oh my God!" she said, "Randy could be the next victim!" Her eyes fearfully searched Daniel's.

Daniel quickly got to his feet. "Stay here for a minute. I'll be right back." He hurried to Lt. Jackson's office. Ben was coming around the corner.

"Slow down, Daniel. What's up?" Ben asked.

"I've got to talk to the lieutenant. The same man who we suspect of being our serial killer employs Randy Kane. He could be the next victim." He rapped on the door, and then opened it without waiting for consent. Ben followed him inside.

Lieutenant Jackson sat behind a large desk and looked up as they entered.

"We need protection for Randy Kane. He works for this guy," Daniel explained, stabbing a finger at the composite sitting on top of a stack of files on the cluttered desk. "The same man we believe is responsible for his brother's death."

Lt. Jackson leaned back in his chair and pulled at his chin. "I agree, but we need to locate him first."

"What do you mean?" Daniel asked.

The older man's eyes narrowed. "Bill Kane just called and said he and his wife still haven't seen or heard from Randy."

"Maybe he found out about his brother and took off to be alone," Ben offered.

"No, I don't buy it. I think he would have gone home for Sara's sake," Daniel said. "The three kids are very close, and the boys very protective of their sister."

Lt. Jackson eyed the detectives. "I want you two to track him down." He glanced at the composite. "I just hope it's not too late."

CHAPTER SEVEN

After stopping at Sara's house, Ben pulled up in front of Daniel's home. "I'll wait out here for you."

"Thanks, Ben. I'll be right back." He got out of the car and Sara slipped out of the backseat.

Taylor stood in the doorway watching them make their way up the walk. "Dad, what's wrong? You still didn't tell me when you called why Sara is staying with us. I mean, I'm glad you are," she quickly added as she looked at her friend. "I just want to know why."

Tears were streaming down Sara's face. "It's bad," she sobbed. She was crying so hard she could barely speak.

Taylor's eyes grew wide and fearful. "What happened?" She put an arm around Sara's thin shoulder. "You're scaring me." She looked at her father. "Dad, what's wrong?"

"Let's get inside, honey." He carried Sara's suitcase to the living room, then set it down. "Taylor, Sara's brother Andy was murdered."

"Oh no!" Taylor cried, then grabbed Sara's hand. "I'm so sorry," she whispered.

101

"Sara is going to stay with us for a while." He turned to Sara. "Try to get some rest. If there's anything you need, please let Taylor know and I'll be home as soon as I can."

She nodded.

"Let's go to my room and get you settled," Taylor said.

"Taylor, would you please walk me to the door?" Daniel asked.

"Sure, Dad. Go on up, Sara, and I'll be there in a minute."

Daniel waited until Sara picked up her suitcase and headed upstairs before walking to the door with Taylor at his side.

"Dad, who would want to kill Andy?"

"I don't know, honey."

She swallowed hard. "Is it the serial killer?"

Daniel was quiet for a minute.

"You think it is?"

He firmly placed his hands on her shoulders. He saw the fear in her eyes. "There's a good possibility that it could be."

"Why can't you catch him?"

"It's not that easy, honey."

"I'm scared, Dad." She shivered.

"Don't be. I'll never let anything happen to you." He wrapped his arms around her and held her close for a minute, then let her go. "I've got to get back to work, sweetie."

"I know."

****

Zoey stood outside Bella's apartment door nervously anticipating what the evening would have in store for her. She pushed the doorbell.

Hunter opened the door, and then stood grinning at her. "Couldn't stay away from me, could you?" His eyes traveled over her body.

"Hunter, for God's sake, stop it! Where's Bella?" she asked, pushing past him. She made her way into the spacious, expensively decorated living room.

"Would you care for a drink?" Hunter asked, sidling up next to her.

He was standing so close she could feel his warm breath on the back of her neck. Her body felt electrified, and she quickly moved away from him. "I asked you where Bella was."

"I'm right here," Bella answered, breezing into the room. She kissed Zoey's cheek, and then slipped her arm through Hunter's. "Did my handsome fiancé offer you a drink?"

"Yes, he did." She looked at Hunter. "I was just about to tell him what I would like."

"What can I get you, Zoey?" Hunter asked with an amused smile.

She looked coldly at him. She hoped he saw the disdain she felt towards him reflected in her eyes. If he did, it didn't seem to faze him. He appeared not to be bothered by her aloofness.

"Mineral water," she answered.

"We do have your favorite wine. You know I always keep it on hand for you," Bella said.

"The mineral water will be fine. I think I may be coming down with something."

"Oh, I hope not," Bella said sympathetically.

"I'll be fine. There's a stomach bug going around. A few of my students have come down with it." She couldn't tell them the real reason she didn't want to drink. For now she could get away with it, but soon they'd know the real reason.

"Daniel couldn't make it tonight?" Bella asked, changing the subject as she motioned her toward the sofa.

"I'm afraid not. He's going to be working most of the night."

She grabbed Bella's hand. "You have heard the news today, haven't you?"

"No. I've been busy all day...why? What's happened?"

Zoey frowned. "They've found another body, and the murder resembles the other four. In fact, some of my students found the body on the way to class this morning."

Bella dramatically placed a hand to her chest. "Oh no! Do they have any leads?"

"The sister of the latest victim gave the police a very good description of a man who could be the murderer. She's a close friend of Daniel's daughter. Nothing concrete, though, but Daniel believes that it's only a matter of time before they catch him."

Hunter handed Zoey a glass of mineral water.

"Thank you," she said, making sure she avoided eye contact with him.

"I fixed you your usual, honey," he said, handing Bella her drink. He seated himself next to Bella, who was sitting on another sofa facing the one Zoey sat on. A large coffee table separated the two sofas. He turned his attention back to Zoey. "What's the motive?"

"Daniel thinks it's drug related."

Hunter frowned. "It doesn't make sense."

"Why not, honey?" Bella asked.

"It doesn't add up. There's got to be more to it. The newscasts have described multiple stab wounds, with one body almost mutilated. Why didn't he just use a gun and shoot them? It would have been cleaner." He sipped at his drink. "No, this guy has a personal vendetta. Has Daniel mentioned anything other than drugs?"

"No. He rarely discusses his work with me. I get my information from the same source as you, Hunter. The local newscasts."

Hunter eyed her suspiciously. "But the newscasts didn't mention a drug connection."

"No matter the motive, I only hope they catch him soon," Bella said. "It's frightening to know there is a serial killer lurking in the city."

Hunter kept his eyes trained on Zoey. She caught his eye, but quickly looked away. She'd taken extra care with her appearance tonight. She had curled her hair just enough so that it fell gently over her shoulders, and the dress she'd chosen clung to her in all the right places. She didn't do it to entice Hunter...it was solely for her own benefit. It would be a few weeks until she began showing, and she intended to make the most of the time she had left before the baby was born. Motherhood would change her, but she was looking forward to it whether it was with or without Daniel. Deep down she already knew that it would be alone. But she intended to give her baby the best life possible. She crossed her legs.

"Yes, it is frightening," Zoey agreed with Bella. "How someone can repeatedly stab another human being is beyond me." She shuddered. "Especially a child."

"How old was he?" Hunter asked.

"Seventeen," she answered. "He was just a kid, with his whole life ahead of him."

"How awful," Bella said.

"I won't rest until they catch him and put him away for good," Zoey said emphatically.

Bella's cook appeared in the doorway.

"Well, ladies, I believe it's time to go in to dinner," Hunter announced.

****

Daniel stepped out of the car, then walked to the door of the bar and quickly disappeared inside. They'd agreed that Ben would stay in the car to keep an eye on the two bars a few doors down in case Randy Kane should enter or leave one of them.

Daniel scanned the room for any sign of Randy Kane before making his way to the bar. The bartender, a thin, twenty something with dirty blond hair tied in a ponytail, glanced curiously at Daniel as he opened two beers. He set the beers in front of a customer, then scooped up the bills the customer threw on the bar and walked over to Daniel. "What can I get you?"

"Nothing, thanks." Daniel took a copy of a picture of Randy Kane from his pocket. "Have you seen him?"

The man took the picture and held it to the light, carefully studying it. "I don't know. Maybe I have and maybe I haven't," he finally answered.

"Well, either you have or you haven't," Daniel replied, instantly despising the young man's attitude.

The bartender propped his elbows on the bar and looked Daniel in the eye. "You must want to find him really bad."

"Yes, I do, but time, unfortunately, is not on my side."

The man inhaled deeply. "Things have been slow around here, if you know what I mean. So, how much is it worth to you?"

Daniel's eyes narrowed. "You expect me to pay you?"

"Why not? Make it worth my while."

"I'm not paying games." Daniel's voice was sharp. "This is not TV. In the real world we don't pay for information," he said, flashing his badge.

"Okay, okay," he said. "But you can't blame a guy for trying. You could have told me you're a cop."

"Do you know him?" Daniel demanded.

He nodded. "Yeah. That's Randy Kane. He has a twin, Andy,

and they usually come in a few times a week."

"Do you serve alcoholic beverages to them?"

The bartender stiffened. "Come on, man. I'm not stupid. They just like to hang out."

"Why here?"

"I don't know." He shrugged. "They have a lot of friends here."

"Now tell me, what does the clientele here have in common with these teenagers?"

"I don't know. They're friendly, likable guys. They don't bother anyone. They come in and shoot a few games of pool. That's all."

"Why don't they hang out at the pool hall instead of coming here?" Daniel asked. "Don't you find that a bit odd?"

"How should I know? I'm not a shrink," he answered sarcastically. "Excuse me. I have a customer."

"I'm not through talking to you."

"I need to wait on my customers. I'll be right back." He moved down the bar, giving Daniel a sideway glance.

Daniel watched him for a few seconds, noticing how the bartender's hand slightly trembled before turning his attention to the seating area of the shabby establishment. It was beyond him why anyone would want to even inhabit this dive. He glanced toward the back of the room. Two elderly men sat slumped in their chairs, oblivious to their surroundings. In the corner, a young man and his companion sat huddled together nursing their beers. Daniel watched the man slip his hand inside the woman's blouse. She seemed oblivious to the public display as the man fondled her breast. Daniel looked away.

He was shocked by the couple's lack of self-respect by allowing others to witness their display of affection that Daniel thought should be private. After Becky's death, he hadn't been with a woman until Zoey. He wasn't a one-night stand kind of guy. He needed to truly connect and know the woman he was making love to. Call it old-fashioned, but he was proud that he'd maintained at least some moral values and beliefs. He was the opposite of Ben, but he knew that Ben was an unhappy man no matter how he tried to convince Daniel otherwise. Ben's one-night stands were meaningless, and Daniel recognized that Ben was lonely and only hooked up to try to ease some of his loneliness. He had loved Clare deeply, and had been blindsided when she'd asked for a divorce and then taken their son and moved to the other side of the country.

When Zoey had broken off with him months ago, Daniel had still remained true to her. He couldn't explain it, but the love he'd shared with her wouldn't just wither and die; he had given her his heart, and that was the ultimate commitment. She was a part of him and always would be, no matter what happened. Their love had bonded them, not just sexually, but in all areas of their lives. He had no desire to take up with someone new. They had been so happy, and then Zoey had changed abruptly. He had had no warning, but he had remained optimistic that she would remember what they had shared and how good they really were together and want to come back to him. Now that she had, as happy as he was, a part of him couldn't let his guard down. His heart had taken a severe blow, and he still needed time to heal and to be able to trust her again. She was pushing too hard and fast, and that bothered him. She hadn't been ready for a commitment before she abruptly left him, but suddenly that's what she wanted. Why? He still intended to take their relationship very slowly, even though he'd love nothing more than to marry her. But a part of him couldn't allow it, at least not yet. He'd suspected she'd broken off with him because of another man, but he never told her that, nor did he intend to.

"I'm back, so what else do you want to know?" the bartender asked with a scowl as he wiped the counter.

Daniel turned back around to face him. "Do you know if either of the Kane boys were dealing drugs?"

"Whoa." He set down the cloth and held his hands up, palms out, in front of Daniel. "If they were, I don't know anything about it. I don't mess with that stuff."

"You never saw them connecting here?" Daniel eyed the man suspiciously, noticing the yellow-stained teeth.

He shook his head. "No way. I told you they came in to shoot pool. That's all."

"Did they ever ask you to buy any drugs?"

"Look, I don't know what you're getting at, but I never saw them making any drug deals, and they didn't offer any drugs to me." He picked the cloth back up. "I don't do drugs."

Daniel observed him closely. "You seem tense."

"I'm not. I just don't like cops." He laid the cloth down again.

"Are you friends with the Kane boys?"

He shrugged again. "I don't know. I suppose so. They're good guys; a little rough around the edges, though."

"Do you associate with them when you're not bartending?"

"No. I'm not really *friends* with them."

Daniel lifted an eyebrow. "I thought you said you were."

The bartender's lips thinned. "You're trying to twist my words around. I only hung around with them when they came in here. I never came in contact with them outside of the bar."

"You're not really much older than they are."

"Old enough to work here."

Daniel leaned in. "I'm going to level with you." He continued staring at him. "What did you say your name was?"

"I didn't, but it's Scott Miles." His eyes narrowed. "I have nothing to hide, so go run my name. I know that's what you are going to do the minute you leave here."

"Well, Scott, you've heard, I'm sure, about the murders committed over the past few weeks."

"Yeah. Who hasn't?"

"This morning Andy Kane's body was found."

"Found like in murdered?" Scott asked hoarsely, as though his throat had suddenly dried out.

Daniel nodded. "That's exactly what I mean."

Scott's face drained of color as he gripped the counter. His knuckles turned white. "I don't believe it," he whispered.

"Now you see why I need to find Randy. His life could be in danger."

"He was in here about four." He thought for a moment. "Yeah, it was about four because I just started work when he came in." He looked suspiciously at Daniel. "Wait a minute. If his twin brother was murdered, he didn't say anything. He would have been broken up."

"He doesn't know."

Scott's face was ashen. "Oh, wow! That's going to blow his mind!" He shook his head. "They were almost always together."

"Did you ask him where his brother was?"

"No. It gets busy when the factories let out, so I didn't get a chance to talk to him. I wish I would have made the time."

"Was he alone when he came in?"

"Yeah. He ordered a cola, like he always does, and then sat at a table in the back. About twenty minutes later, some guy came in. He stood at the door and looked around. I kept my eye on him since he wasn't a regular. He spotted Randy, went to the back, and sat with him."

"Do you know if they left together?"

"I have no clue. Like I said, it was getting busy and I didn't see either of them leave."

"Can you give me a description of the guy you saw with Randy?"

"Yeah. He was dressed like some hotshot lawyer or executive. You know, the three piece suit deal. He looked out of place in here dressed like that." His eyebrows drew together. "He's probably in his mid-thirties."

"Anything else?"

"Let me think." His eyebrows drew together. "Oh, yeah!" he said. "He had a neatly trimmed mustache and wire-rimmed glasses. The glasses didn't look right on him. Real geeky looking."

"Would you recognize him if you saw him again?"

"Yeah, I think so. You don't forget someone like that in a place like this."

Daniel took a smaller version of the composite from his pocket. "Is this him?"

Scott took the picture and held it to the light. "Yeah, that's the guy." He frowned. "This is just a drawing. Do you think this is the guy who killed all those people? Did he kill Andy?"

Daniel ignored his question. "Did Randy tell you where he was going?"

"No, like I told you, I didn't have time to talk to him, and I didn't see him leave."

"That's right, you did. Do you know any of his hangouts?"

He was thoughtful for a minute. "Once in a while the bar down the street, but mostly they liked to come here. Like I said, they love shooting pool, and that bar has a rough crowd."

"The other bar allows minors, too?"

Scott flushed. "Hey, as long as they behave and aren't trying to get someone to score them a drink, I don't see the harm in them coming in to shoot a few games of pool."

Daniel eyed him carefully. "Just so they aren't being served any alcohol."

"I'm not that stupid," Scott said emphatically.

"I believe you, Scott," Daniel answered. "Do you know any of Randy's friends?"

"He doesn't really have any close friends that I know of. Andy and him are real loners. No, I take that back. They started hanging out with Asher Michaels. He comes in sometimes with them, but never by himself. I don't know him too well."

"I appreciate your help, Scott. Here's my card," he said, putting it into Scott's hand. "If this guy should come back, or you see him anywhere, please call immediately. The same goes for Randy. If he comes in, call the station and try to keep him here until the police get here."

Scott nodded.

CHAPTER EIGHT

Sara lay sprawled across Taylor's bed. "I just can't seem to get it into my head that I'm never going to see Andy again. It feels like a bad dream." She looked at Taylor. "Do you know what I mean?"

"Yes. I know exactly how you feel. I felt that way about my mother when she died. Even though she hadn't been a part of my life for a long time, I still couldn't believe that I wouldn't see her again. Dad used to take me to visit her every week. I guess I thought someday she'd come knocking at the door." Taylor looked sympathetically at her. "Is there anything I can do, Sara? I know everybody always says that, but I would really do anything if it would help you."

"I know you would, but just letting me stay here means more than you'll ever know." Her eyes brimmed with fresh tears "This has been such a weird day." She sat up, bringing the pillow to her chest. "I can't believe that my parents finally realize they have a drinking problem and want to clean up their lives." She shook her head. "It's too bad Andy had to die before they realized it."

"I know," Taylor said softly. "But at least they did."

"Yeah, at least that's something." A tear rolled down her cheek. "I'm worried sick about Randy. I hope your dad calls soon with some news."

Taylor put an arm around her. "I'm sure Randy will be found safe and sound."

Sara sniffed. "I hope so. I just want this nightmare to be over, and I want Randy to be safe," she sobbed.

Taylor wondered how Sara would be able to survive the next few days. Andy's funeral would be difficult for everyone to get through. And God forbid if something did happen to Randy, too. She bit her bottom lip as a chill ran down her spine.

****

"Are you sure you won't have some wine, Zoey?" Hunter asked.

Zoey shook her head. "No, thank you."

"Well, I'll have a little more," Bella said, holding out her glass.

Hunter looked curiously at Zoey as he refilled Bella's glass.

"The meal was delicious, Bella," Zoey raved. "I wish I could cook like that."

"You and me both," Bella replied. "I'm grateful to have Avis. She's a wonderful cook."

Hunter cocked an eye. "I suppose after the wedding my talents won't be welcomed in the kitchen," he joked.

"No, my darling, frozen dinners aren't much to my liking. But I assure you I will find a more suitable outlet for your talents."

He laughed as he lifted his wine glass to his lips. "And I promise you that you will thoroughly enjoy my talents." He kept an eye trained on Zoey to gage her reaction.

Bella's face reddened. "I think we'd better stop this line of conversation or we might embarrass Zoey."

"I think you're the one who's embarrassed, dear," Hunter said, winking at her. "Zoey has never struck me as the type who embarrasses easily."

She stood up. "Nonetheless, I think I'll end it here and go to the kitchen and let Avis know that we're ready for coffee and dessert. Why don't you two go into the living room and I'll join you in a few minutes."

"Shall we?" Hunter stood up, then walked over to Zoey and pulled her chair out for her. He gently took her elbow and led her to the living room, where he seated himself next to her on the sofa. "How's your love life lately?" he whispered into her ear.

Zoey stiffened. "My love life, as well as all areas of my life, is none of your business," she answered curtly.

"Just as I thought." He grinned. "I warned you...once you've had me, baby, no other man will ever be good enough for you." He ran his fingertips gently down her arm.

She grimaced, pushing his hand away. "You know, Hunter, you've got a serious ego problem. I really feel sorry for you. You'll never experience true love because you're too much in love with yourself." She looked into his eyes. "And for your information, you aren't as good as you think."

Hunter chuckled. "You can say what you like," he replied as his eyes wandered up and down the length of her slender legs, "but I know that you will always desire me and only me." He shifted until his thigh was pressed next to hers. "Admit it. You're madly in love with me."

"I've done a lot of thinking lately, and I don't think I ever truly loved you, Hunter. Not the kind of enduring love that counts." She stared at him. "I was taken in by your looks and charm. But now I see what a fool I was, because there is nothing inside. You're an empty vessel." She laughed softly. "Someday, my friend, your looks will be gone. Then you'll have nothing because you're incapable of loving anyone."

"Keep talking, but I know the truth. You'll always desire only me." He smiled. "When you want a real man to fuck, you know how to reach me." He abruptly stood up. "Please tell Bella that I will return shortly. I'm going to the den to make a business call."

Zoey watched him exit the room, wondering how she would ever convince him that what was once between them was over. At first she'd only decided to cut him loose because of her overwhelming guilt, but suddenly it dawned on her that she really did feel nothing at all for him. The realization seeped into her mind, filling her entire soul with the knowledge so deep and true that it shocked her. She felt absolutely *nothing* for Hunter Tucker. All the pain and hurt he had caused her was now replaced with Daniel's secure, comforting love. She knew that Daniel would never hurt or deceive her. He was incapable of it, and no other man would ever be as faithful and committed to her as Daniel was. She knew that buried deep inside she'd always loved him; it had just gotten lost somewhere during her infatuation stage with Hunter. Yes, that was the proper term for what she had felt for Hunter…infatuation. It was so different from love. Infatuation eventually faded and died. But the love she'd shared with Daniel was enduring, and grew only stronger with time. She wanted to spend the rest of her life with him.

She looked up when Bella entered the room. A dark shadow passed through her consciousness as she anticipated Daniel and Bella's reactions to her past with Hunter. She was aware that she could lose the only two people who had ever mattered to her. She didn't have to tell them, but her conscience wouldn't let her keep a secret of this magnitude. Besides, Hunter could expose their affair if anything ever happened between him and Bella.

She knew he wouldn't hesitate to destroy her happiness. He was evil.

Bella set a beautiful silver tray on the coffee table. "Where did my handsome fiancé go?" she asked.

"He said he had to make a business call."

Bella frowned as she poured the coffee. "That man can't tear himself away from his work for even one evening." She handed Zoey a cup of coffee.

"Thank you." Zoey sipped at her coffee. "You've never mentioned his work. What exactly does he do?"

"He has many investments. I don't ask too many questions. You know how I am when it comes to business."

"Haven't you ever wanted to run your company, Bella?" Zoey asked.

She shook her head. "I think my father would have loved nothing more, but I just had no interest in it. Thank God he had the foresight to make certain that after his death the company would still run smoothly without my involvement."

Zoey pursed her lips. "That's where you and I differ. I'd want to be there knowing every little detail."

Bella threw her head back and laughed. "I know you would. And you'd probably do a wonderful job." She looked slyly at her friend. "But you also know that deep down you wouldn't be happy sitting in some corporate office all day long. You'd need to be up dancing around. You'd be lucky if you could sit still for more than five minutes at a time."

Zoey grinned. "I suppose you're right. I'd go crazy sitting at a desk all day long. Besides, dancing and teaching dance makes me happy. It might not make me rich, but as long as it pays the bills that's all I care about."

Bella nodded. "I wholeheartedly agree. And it appears that

you and I, my friend, have both found the perfect men that have added to that happiness. They accept us just the way we are."

Zoey became quiet. She sat sipping her coffee thinking about what Bella had just said.

"Why so quiet all of a sudden?" Bella asked.

"Nothing," she smiled weakly. "I was just thinking about Daniel."

"I'm so happy that you two are back together, Zoey. Even though you tried to hide it, I knew you were miserable without him." Her eyes brightened. "Maybe in the not too distant future, we will be celebrating your wedding."

Zoey sighed heavily. "Not in the near future, I'm afraid. That is a topic we haven't discussed. One that Daniel definitely does not want to discuss."

"Oh?" Bella's eyebrows shot up. "I thought that was all Daniel wanted."

"He did then, but since we've gotten back together he doesn't seem to be in such a hurry."

Bella frowned. "Well, you did break his heart."

Zoey sighed. "I know. I hope someday he'll be able to forgive me unconditionally."

"He will," Bella assured her. "He loves you."

****

The ringing phone irritated Bob Michaels. "Asher, get the phone!" he bellowed after the fifth ring. When he received no response, he threw his hammer aside and grabbed the phone. "Hello."

"I would like to speak to Asher Michaels, please."

"May I ask who's calling?" Bob Michaels asked suspiciously. Normally his son received personal calls on his cell phone. Rarely did Asher receive a call on the landline. But then this caller's voice sounded older. He hoped Asher hadn't gotten himself into trouble.

"Yes, this is his employer. It's urgent that I speak with him immediately."

He frowned. As far as he knew Asher wasn't employed, even though he'd hounded his son for months to find another job after the pizza place he'd worked at had closed down. "Sure. I'll get him." He walked down the hall to Asher's bedroom. Loud music blared from the other side of the door. Michaels felt his blood pressure rise as he pounded on the door. Seconds later the music stopped and Asher opened the door.

Asher ran a hand through his rumpled hair. "Sorry. Was the music too loud?"

"Yes," his father grumbled. "But that's not why I'm here. You have a call," he said, handing the cordless to his son.

Asher took the phone. "Who is it?"

"He said he's your boss. Congrats on the job." Bob turned on his heel and walked back down the hall. He didn't see the fear in his son's eyes or the way his body stiffened.

Asher closed his bedroom door and sat on the edge of his bed. "Hello," he mumbled into the receiver.

"I don't like to be kept waiting. Time is valuable to me."

"Sorry. I was busy."

"Was that your father who answered the phone?" he demanded.

The sharpness of his voice unnerved Asher. "Yes."

"Did you tell him my name?"

"No. He didn't ask."

"Make sure you don't mention my name to anyone."

Beads of perspiration broke out on his forehead. "I won't, but—"

"No buts," Mr. D interrupted. "Are you still seeing that Kane girl?"

"So, do I have the job or what?"

"I asked you a question. Are you seeing the Kane girl?"

"No, we had a fight. Why?"

"You have the job."

"When do I start?" Asher asked, wondering why his boss had asked about Sara.

"Have you heard the news about Andy Kane?" he asked.

"No," Asher replied, wondering why Mr. D hadn't answered his question, and now assumed he was going to tell him that he'd fired Andy. Asher felt bad for Andy. He'd wait until Mr. D told him the news, and then he'd speak up in Andy's defense about the shortage. That's the least he could do. If he got pissed that Andy had brought him along he'd just tell him to shove the job if Andy no longer worked for him. Of course he'd be more tactful when he refused the employment. His friendship with Andy and Randy meant more than a job.

"I know you were with Andy yesterday when he made the delivery, so don't try to deny it."

"I wasn't going to," Asher said quickly. "We made the delivery yesterday, and he said he was meeting you to give you the envelope. I wanted to go with him when he met you to explain—"

"Explain what? That he's a fuck-up who doesn't obey orders?" Mr. D said, cutting Asher off. "His body was found this morning."

"What!" Asher choked. "He's dead? How? Did he crash his bike?" His voice shook.

"Like the others...stabbed."

It took a minute for the words to sink in. When they finally did, fear gripped Asher as he realized what Mr. D was saying. "By the serial killer?" His body trembled and he felt sick to his stomach.

"What do you think?" the man sarcastically asked. "Someone is always watching. Don't ever forget that."

Asher ran a shaky hand over his chin. "Wait a minute—"

"No one double-crosses me."

Asher's palms grew moist, almost causing him to drop the phone. "I...I don't want the job," he stammered. "I changed my mind."

Mr. D laughed. "I'm afraid that the choice is no longer yours."

"What do you mean?" Asher swallowed hard.

"I don't think I need to explain myself. You know exactly what I mean."

The tone of Mr. D's voice sent an icy chill down Asher's spine. His breath came in spurts. He knew exactly what the man meant. He had to think quickly. "I'll go to the police. I'll—"

"Listen, punk, who do you think will believe you? You don't even know my name."

"But I—"

"Shut up! You seem to forget who's in charge here!" he snarled. "You'll do exactly as I say. If you don't, you'll regret it. Do I make myself clear?"

Asher inhaled deeply. "Yeah, I guess so."

"You *guess* so?"

Asher cringed at the threatening tone. "I mean I'll do what you say."

"All right, then." He paused. "I want you to find Sara Kane for me."

"How can I do that? She's not talking to me." He swallowed hard. Why would he want Sara? No matter, there was no way in hell he'd let this monster get his hands on Sara.

"Figure it out! I want you to find her and bring her to the warehouse by midnight."

"What if she won't come with me?"

"Make sure that she does, because if she refuses, you may end up just like your friend."

****

"What's up?" Ben Wilson asked as Daniel got back into the car.

"I think we're on to something," Daniel replied. "Randy Kane was here earlier today with a guy who fit the same description Stephanie Rinehart and Sara Kane gave us." He looked at Ben. "Anyone suspicious in or out of the bar down the street?"

"No. Only a few went in and a couple came out. Want to check the warehouse again?"

Daniel hesitated. "Do you really think he's that stupid? Besides, we have a car patrolling the area. No one's come in or out of the place." His eyebrows furrowed.

Ben scowled. "Face it, Daniel, he's been one step ahead of us all the way. He's probably thinking that the warehouse is the last place we'd expect him to show up. So that's where he'll go. He may be getting in there a different way. The patrol car only sees from the highway."

"I don't know how he'd get in from the back. It'd be quite a hike. Last I knew it was all overgrown. I don't think kids even go there anymore to party like they did a few years ago. Besides, didn't the owners install a fence to keep the kids out?"

"Yeah, but fences won't keep someone out if they really are determined to get in." Ben pulled on his chin. "It'd be a perfect place to hide a car in the underbrush and sneak in. No one would see from the road."

"Yeah, maybe," Daniel said quietly. Then he was struck by a thought. "Yeah, what you said makes sense. Let's get over there."

****

Randy aimlessly wandered the north side of town looking for Andy. He had to meet Mr. D. in two hours, and he was scared. His earlier delivery had accused Mr. D of ripping him off and had made a substantial deduction, which Randy knew he'd be expected to replace in short order. He wished there was some way he could get hold of the money before the meeting, but no one he knew had that kind of money. If only the delivery had been made before he'd met Mr. D at the bar. Then he would have been in a public place when he explained what had happened.

He thought about the meeting. He'd been surprised when his boss had asked to meet him, because never before had the boss met any of them in a public setting. Why today? All Mr. D had talked about was Andy and how he'd stiffed him, and how they'd mutually figured out a way for Andy's debt to be repaid.

Would his boss be as generous with him? He thought about blowing off the meeting until he had all of the money. No, that wouldn't work. If he didn't show up, Mr. D would only hunt him down. And he didn't want to even think about what the consequences would be. He was worried about Andy because he hadn't come home last night, and when he'd mentioned that to Mr. D the man had blown him off. Not that Andy always found his way home, but when he didn't, Randy usually knew about it. They always had one another's backs. When he woke up this morning, he'd assumed he'd glance over at his brother's bed and see him fast asleep burrowed under his blankets. When he hadn't, an uneasy feeling had settled over him.

He was tired and hungry. When he left this morning, he hadn't even taken time for a bite of food. He had been carrying almost ten grand around with him all day, except for the missing five hundred. He smiled as he thought about what he could do with the money. He could just disappear into thin air and live a life of ease. Now wouldn't that be nice? Yeah, his fantasies were nice, but in reality Mr. D would scour the world until he found him. He drew a deep breath.

"Dammit!" he muttered as he walked over to his motorcycle. He stood admiring it, remembering when he and Andy had finally saved enough money to buy their bikes. They could hardly believe it when the day had finally come. They, along with Asher Michaels, had spent countless hours tinkering until the bikes were in mint condition. He got on his bike, started it up, and then sped off into the night.

****

"So what have you two lovely ladies been discussing in my absence?" Hunter asked, walking back into the room.

"Just girl talk," Bella replied, smiling brightly at him. "The topics which would bore you to tears, I'm afraid."

Zoey felt sick to her stomach as she watched Bella's eyes literally light up at the sight of him.

"I can't wait until I can officially claim you for my bride," he said. He laid a gentle hand on her arm, but kept a sharp eye trained on Zoey.

"I can't either," she gushed. "Did you take care of your business so you can spend some time with us?"

"There's a minor problem with one of the investors in my new enterprise." He frowned. "I'm afraid I'll have to leave for a short time."

"No, Hunter, not tonight," she replied with a pout. "Can't someone else handle it?"

He shook his head. "I'm sorry, honey, but I'm the only one

who can take care of it. I promise to return as soon as I can." He kissed her cheek, and then abruptly left the room.

"What could be so important this time of night?" Zoey asked suspiciously.

"I don't know," Bella said. "It must be something that can't wait until morning or he wouldn't leave."

"Does he do this a lot?" Zoey asked.

She sighed. "Unfortunately, yes, but it can't be helped. He's in and out all the time. This is a new enterprise, and it means the world to him. I think that's why he insists on handling it himself." She looked at Zoey. "I have no right to insist that he not go."

"I suppose," she answered.

"What's the matter, Zoey?" Her eyes searched Zoey's face. "You've been acting odd all night. You don't approve of Hunter, do you?"

Zoey shook her head slowly back and forth. "It shouldn't matter to you whether I approve or disapprove of him, Bella."

"But it does matter to me, Zoey." She pursed her lips. "Is something else bothering you?"

"Now isn't the time to discuss it." She set her coffee cup down. "I should be going."

"You're scaring me, Zoey. Do you know something about Hunter? If you do, then please tell me what it is," she said in a shaky voice. "Don't I have the right to know? As your friend?"

"I can't...not this way...not now." She avoided looking into Bella's probing eyes. She needed to get out of there.

"Zoey, I'm pleading with you. Please tell me if there is something I should know about Hunter. Is he cheating on me?"

Her face flushed. "I can't talk about it right now." She stood up. "I've got to go." She brushed Bella's cheek with her lips. "I'll call you tomorrow."

Bella grabbed her arms. "Zoey, what's wrong? I'm frightened. Please talk to me."

Zoey smiled weakly. "Nothing's wrong. I'm just feeling a bit under the weather. I told you I wasn't feeling well."

Bella released her. "Why don't I believe that?" Her eyes searched Zoey's face.

****

Randy Kane lit a cigarette as he waited for Mr. D. He'd tried quitting smoking, but he always went back. Especially when he was nervous. He wondered why Mr. D had asked him to meet him five miles up the road at a smaller abandoned warehouse. It was an inconvenience to get his bike through the tangled weeds in the overgrown path, and then he had to go another quarter mile around the back. He was out of breath and panting when he finally reached his destination. Hopefully the cigarette would calm his nerves a little and help him to relax. The place gave him the creeps.

Silently he practiced the speech, which he hoped would convince Mr. D that he hadn't stolen any money, and give him the same kind of leniency he'd extended to his brother. He looked at his scratched arms. He was husky, but not overweight. He slicked his black hair back away from his brow, revealing a set of dark eyes spaced perfectly in his handsome face. He and Andy were identical except for their weight and height, with Andy fifteen pounds lighter and four inches taller. Andy and he were almost inseparable...always had been. If one decided to do something, the other usually followed suit. It was the same with this job. They were hanging out one night at the bar they often frequented to shoot pool when a well-dressed man approached them. It had never occurred to either of them why a man dressed so expensively would inhabit a bar most would consider a dive.

126

After the man told them how much money they could make, it didn't take long to convince them that this was their golden opportunity to fulfill some of their dreams. Like eventually buying new bikes. Actually, it had been Randy who had taken the initiative and had talked Andy into it. Their minor run-ins with the law had Andy worried, since they were both on probation. If their probation were violated in any way, they would be sent to jail. Andy had always been the worrier of the two, and Randy was the risk taker. Randy believed in living for the moment and never worried about the consequences. Usually he managed to get out of any difficult situation, and knew if he played his cards right, he would get out of this, too.

"I see you made it, Kane," a deep voice said from somewhere in the shadows behind him. He carried a bright lantern and shined it in Randy's eyes.

Randy turned, startled. "Yeah," he said shuffling his feet. "Look, Mr. D, I didn't take the money, but since you think I did, I'll try to come up with it as soon as I can. I need a little time."

The man laughed. "I can't believe that you boys think I'm that stupid." He laid a hand on Randy's shoulder. "Here I am being a nice guy offering you boys the chance to earn some good honest money, and look what happens. I get ripped off." His eyebrows knitted together. "Is no one honest at all today?"

"I swear I didn't rip you off," Randy insisted. "I didn't touch the envelope. I never know how much money is inside. You know they're always sealed. I only know what the guy said when he gave it to me. Maybe it's all there. It's still sealed. Count it." He pulled the envelope from his front jean pocket and thrust it at Mr. D.

Mr. D took the envelope and tore it open. He set the lantern down and squatted quickly, counting the cash.

127

Randy waited expectantly, relieved that the glaring light was out of his eyes. "Well?"

"Five hundred missing." The man shook his head. "Now what do you think would be a fitting punishment?" He shoved the envelope into his sport coat pocket and stood back up, bringing the lantern with him.

"I said I'd pay you back. Just take it out of what I have coming." He thrust his chin out. "Look, I don't need this shit! You can shove this job up your ass!" He turned and started to walk away.

"Kane, let me think about this for a moment."

Randy turned to face him. "So, what's the deal?" he asked.

"How about a compromise?"

"I don't follow you."

"You will. I can't let you walk away. You know that, don't you? You can never quit. You know too much."

"I promise I'll keep my mouth shut. Who would I tell?" he asked sarcastically. "I'd only be getting myself in trouble. So as of now I officially quit."

"No, you don't quit." He slipped his hand into his pocket.

"Right. So now you think you own me?" Randy watched as Mr. D slowly brought his hand out. His eye caught the glint of a shiny blade. "No way!" he screamed as he lunged for the knife, knocking the lantern to the ground as he tried to wrestle it out of the man's tight grip.

Mr. D grabbed Randy's wrist with one hand, then with the other swiftly thrust the knife into the boy before he could utter another word.

****

Hunter walked into the living room and over to the sofa where Bella sat reading a magazine. She looked up and flashed him a bright smile. "Did you get the problem taken care of?"

He bent over, and then kissed her cheek. "Yes." He sat next to her. "It won't be long until my new investment begins paying off, and even more than I dreamed." He put an arm around her. "Now we can concentrate on the wedding."

She grabbed his hand. "I can't wait, Hunter, but a part of me is very scared."

"Why, honey?" he asked softly. "Are you having a change of heart about marrying me?"

"Of course not. I'm the luckiest woman in the world. It just seems too good to be true, as though I'm dreaming." She sighed. "I'm frightened that something will go wrong."

"Nothing will go wrong." He gazed into her eyes. "I promise you that." He touched the engagement ring on her finger. "When I placed that ring on your finger, I pledged my faithfulness and love to you and only you." He tilted her head, and then kissed her deeply. "No more worrying."

She rested her head on his shoulder. "You make everything seem so perfect. I feel so safe and protected when I'm with you."

He bent his head and looked into her eyes. "But I suspect that something else is bothering you. It's not just pre-wedding jitters, is it?"

"I can't keep anything from you, can I?" she admitted.

"No, you can't. Those beautiful eyes of yours are telling. Now, what is it, Bella?"

She frowned. "Zoey was in such a strange mood tonight. She said she had something to tell me, but couldn't. Did she say anything to you, Hunter?"

"No. But then of course, why would she? We chat, but I really know very little about her. I doubt I would be her choice for a confidant. After all, I barely know her, and you've known her for years." His brow furrowed. "I did notice that she was unusually quiet tonight." He shrugged. "Possibly Daniel and she are having problems."

"I don't think that's it." She lifted a shoulder. "Well, I suppose if it's important, she'll eventually tell me."

"I wouldn't lose any sleep over it."

She smiled. "I don't intend to. Instead, I'm going to focus all of my energy on something more preferable than sleep." She stood and took his hand and led him to the bedroom.

CHAPTER NINE

Ben and Daniel jumped out of the patrol car and made their way to the entrance of the warehouse. They held their guns in position. The moon cast an eerie glow over the old, deteriorating building. Cautiously they entered the building through the partially open door. They listened, but heard nothing.

"Cover me," Ben whispered, feeling his way along the wall. After a few minutes of silence, he spoke again. "All clear."

Daniel turned on his flashlight and flashed it around the room. "It doesn't look like anyone's been here recently. I guess we were wrong."

"Let's check out the rest of the place anyway," Ben said, shining his flashlight in the opposite direction.

Daniel trained his light on the weather beaten stained floor. He carefully shined it back and forth across the floor. Something caught his eye. He bent down to examine it more closely. "Ben, get over here! I've got something."

"What'd you find?"

"If it's what I think it is, then we may be on to something after all."

131

Ben examined the area of the floor where Daniel was squatted. "It looks like blood," he said. "It's fresh, too."

Daniel looked closer. "It's a trail."

"Let's see where it leads."

They followed the trail for a few feet, and then it abruptly ended. "What the hell?" Daniel looked at his partner.

"We'd better call it in and get a team over here. It looks like whoever was bleeding either got some help, or the attacker dragged the victim on something," Ben stated.

"Another long night," Daniel stated.

"Looks like it." Ben stood up. "I think my theory might have been right after all," he stated as he walked toward the back of the building.

Daniel followed him. He stopped in front of a door, or what was left of one. He walked through it, and the first thing he noticed was the flattened grass from tire tracks. "Dammit," he muttered. "What you said is exactly what he did."

"He must have laughed his ass off committing murder right under our noses." Ben's jaw tightened.

"The blood looks too fresh to be Andy Kane's," Daniel stated. He looked at Ben.

"I don't even want to think that, Daniel."

"We have to, Ben. This blood could be Randy Kane's."

****

Mr. D rummaged through his closet for a shirt. He grabbed one, put it on, and slowly buttoned it. He picked up a burner cell phone and dialed Asher Michael's telephone number.

Asher picked up the phone on the first ring. "Yeah."

"Michaels, we have a change in plans for tonight."

Asher took a deep breath. "I didn't get hold of Sara yet."

"You'd better meet me at the old train depot and have the

Kane girl with you!" he ordered. "If you're not there, I'll find you, and when I do, I don't think I need to paint a picture for you."

Asher blew his breath out. "I'll be there."

****

Sara slowly ran a brush through her long hair. "I guess there is some good even in the most horrible situations," she said.

"What do you mean?" Taylor asked.

Sara laid the hairbrush down. "Well, look at my parents. Andy's death seems to have opened their eyes to what's wrong in their lives. I don't know…." Her voice trailed off.

"Why don't you try to get some sleep?"

"I don't think I can. I still think I'm in the middle of a bad dream."

Taylor couldn't bear the pain her friend was going through. She wished she could find the words, any words, to ease her pain even just a little. But she knew there were none. She gave Sara a hug. "I'm always here for you," she said.

"I know. I don't know what I'd do without you and your dad."

The phone rang. "It's probably my dad," Taylor said.

"Wouldn't he call your cell?"

"You're right. Probably a telemarketer. That's why we still have the landlines." She grabbed it. "Hello?"

"Taylor, please don't hang up. It's Asher. I don't know your cell number, so I looked up your home number," he said quickly. "Listen, is Sara there? She's not answering her cell phone."

She hesitated as she looked at Sara. "Yes she is, Asher. She turned her phone off."

"Please ask her to talk to me."

"I'll try." She raised an eyebrow as she looked at her friend

133

and held out the phone.

Sara shook her head.

Taylor waited a few seconds before responding. "I'm sorry, Asher, but she doesn't want to talk to anyone right now."

"Please try to get her to talk to me, Taylor. I know I acted like a jerk, but I'm really sorry. I just want to talk to her. I'm busted up about Andy's death and everything. He was my best friend," he choked.

Taylor heard the genuine pain and sorrow in his voice. She felt sorry for him. "I'll see what I can do, Asher." She held her hand over the receiver again as she spoke to Sara. "He's really upset. He just wants to talk to you. He's sorry for the way he acted." Her eyes misted. "He's crying."

Sara frowned. "I don't know."

Taylor eyed her sharply. "You know you still care about him."

"But it doesn't mean I forgive him." She took the phone from Taylor. "What do you want, Asher?" Her voice was chilly.

"I'm really sorry about Andy. I still can't believe it." He hesitated for a few seconds. "Sara, I'm real sorry for what I said to you that night. I didn't mean it." His voice trembled. "Please say you forgive me. I am *so* sorry."

A tear slid down Sara's cheek. "Asher, I'm scared. There's too much for me to sort out right now. I don't know why all this is happening," she sobbed. "And I'm worried sick about Randy."

"I've been trying to reach him. We were supposed to get together, but he never showed. I didn't know why until I heard about Andy. I'm still in shock myself."

"Randy doesn't know."

"What? Where is he?"

Sara shuddered. "The police have been searching all day and

night for him." She began to sob. "No one can find him."

"He's missing?"

"Yes."

"I'm so sorry, Sara. What can I do? I need to do something."

"Just let me know if he shows up at your house. Please, Asher."

"Of course I will," he answered. "I want to be there for you," he whispered. "I promise never to hurt you again."

"We can talk later," she said softly. "I miss you."

****

Beads of perspiration broke out on Asher's forehead as he paced back and forth in his bedroom. He had to figure out a plan, because he definitely would not take Sara to Mr. D. That wasn't even a possibility. Asher knew he was probably signing his own death warrant, but that was a chance he had to take. He was worried about Randy. It would have made sense that he'd gone off somewhere by himself to mourn his brother, but if he didn't even know that Andy was dead, then it made absolutely no sense at all. He tried Randy's cell again, but it immediately went to voice mail. Asher had always considered himself as tough, but his emotions started to break down. He was mourning the loss of one friend, worried about the safety of another, and terrified that Sara's life was now also in grave danger. What had he gotten himself into? He quit pacing and sat on the edge of his bed. He put his face in his hands and began to sob.

****

Ben looked quizzically at Lt. Jackson. "Did anything come back yet?"

"No." The lieutenant leaned back in his chair. "Prepare for a long night, gentlemen."

Daniel poured himself a fresh cup of coffee. "When will the

report be back on the blood sample?"

"Should be any minute now. Did you two have any luck tracking down Randy Kane?"

"You mean in case the blood isn't his?" Daniel asked, but didn't wait for an answer. "No, we didn't. It's as though he disappeared into thin air. We can only hope that he shows up."

Lt. Jackson shook his head. "I have a hunch that if we don't find this boy soon, it'll be too late."

"I've got to call home to check on the girls," Daniel said.

"Go ahead," Jackson said.

Daniel stepped away from Jackson's desk, pulled out his cell phone, and pressed Taylor's number. She answered on the fifth ring. "Hello," she said drowsily.

"Hi, honey. It looks like I'm going to be here for a while. Is everything all right?"

"Yeah. Sara's sleeping. She cried herself to sleep. Did you find Randy?"

"Not yet."

"Dad, do you think he's okay?"

"I don't know, honey. I hope so."

"Dad, he has to be all right." She paused. "I'm scared."

"I know you are. I'll be home as soon as I can. Did you lock up and put the alarm on?"

"Yes."

"Good. Try to get some sleep. If there's any news I'll let you know."

"Okay. Oh, I almost forgot. Zoey called. She said she didn't want to bother you if you were still at work, but said it's important and to call her no matter what time you get home."

"Okay, honey. You get some rest now and I'll see you later." After he hung up, he quickly dialed Zoey's number. "Hi, Zoey.

Taylor said you wanted to talk to me. What's up?"

"I just need to discuss a few things, Daniel."

"You sound upset. Have you been crying?"

"No, I'm just on edge. I have some news and I'm not sure of your reaction."

"Can you tell me now?" He glanced toward the open door and watched a detective walk quickly to Lt. Jackson and hand him a folder.

"Can you come over?"

"I'd love to but I'm still at the station, and it looks like I'll be here most of the night."

"It can wait. Why don't you give me a call tomorrow after you've had some sleep, Daniel?"

"Okay. I'll see you tomorrow, then." He paused. "Are you sure you'll be all right?"

"I'll be fine."

"Okay, then."

"Goodnight, Daniel."

Daniel put his phone back into his pocket as he walked back over to the lieutenant's desk. "Anything?" he asked.

"No." Lt. Jackson removed his glasses.

"We've searched this entire city looking for Randy Kane." Daniel's brow creased. "Except for one area. We haven't checked the lake area. The teens are always hanging around down there."

"It's late. Do you think he'd be there?"

Daniel shrugged. "I don't know. Maybe someone will be hanging around who has seen him today."

The lieutenant's phone rang and he answered on the first ring. Daniel's ears perked up when he heard Lt. Jackson greet the caller as Mr. Kane. Hopefully Randy was home, and he could at the very least offer Sara that news.

"Has Randy showed up?" Daniel asked.

"I'm afraid not. Mr. Kane was hoping we had some news."

"How are they holding up?"

"He said they're not giving up hope." He shook his head. "I don't know how anyone could bear what that poor family has had to deal with today." He glanced at the clock. "Or I should say yesterday."

Daniel nodded. "I know."

"We've got all of the abandoned warehouses covered. Why don't you two take a run out to the lake area? I'll let you know if anything new develops on this end or if the report comes back."

Daniel turned to Ben, who had just ended a phone conversation. "We're going to check the lake front area," he said.

"Good idea."

They walked to the car and Ben tossed the keys to Daniel. "You drive this time," he said, climbing into the passenger seat. He stretched his long legs.

"Had to cancel your plans for tonight, huh, stud?"

Ben scowled. "Yeah, and let me tell you, it was not an easy thing to do. I was going to wine and dine her."

"Anyone I know?" Daniel asked.

"I don't think so. Becca Rhodes. I met her last weekend at a bar on the south side."

"Was she upset with you for canceling?"

"No, she took it very well. She said she'd ask a friend to do something with her tonight. I told her we could try for next weekend."

"What's wrong with tomorrow night?"

"She's seeing someone she has a standing date with."

Daniel laughed. "You sure know how to pick them, Ben."

"If you saw her you'd go after her, too," Ben stated.

Daniel shook his head. "Not me."

"Remember, variety is the spice of life."

"Not in my life. I want only one woman."

"I thought you had her. Still not sure about Zoey?"

"I don't know how I feel. I love her. That never changed. I just can't fully trust her."

"Doesn't sound so different than Clare and me." He paused. "Does it?"

Daniel thought about that for a minute. "I hear what you're saying. You never saw it coming with Clare. And I never expected Zoey to abruptly break off. In my case, though, I don't know if she cheated or not." He glanced at Ben. "If circumstances suddenly changed, would you ever take Clare back?"

"No. Not in a million years. What she did is unforgivable. I could never trust her again. All I'd spend my time doing would be wondering if she was cheating. You've got to trust your head and not your heart, Daniel.

"Now that is easier said than done. That's why I'm taking my time and trying not to let my emotions rule me."

"Yeah, I know what you mean. Maybe someday I'll settle down again. But I just can't seem to find the right woman. At least one I can trust."

"Well, you won't find her in those bars you inhabit."

"I know. They're just a diversion. I'm not ready for anything permanent. After what Clare did to me, it's going to be a long time until I'm ready to make another commitment...if ever."

"I get that," Daniel said. "Have you heard from Josh recently?"

"No. He's been busy with his baseball team. He calls when he hits a home run, and I have to visualize it when I should be cheering from the stands," he replied bitterly.

Daniel felt sorry for him. He knew he'd be just as bitter if his circumstances with Becky had been different and she'd taken Taylor across the country far away from him. He couldn't imagine not seeing Taylor every day. "How's Clare doing? Is she easing up any on you?"

"She has a new man in her life." He blinked hard. "Josh is getting very close to him. They do all the things together that he and I should be doing. She loves telling me all about it and rubbing it in. She's spiteful. Here I was the one who was faithful, she cheated, and she gets my kid and my money."

"You know how Josh feels about you, Ben. No one can take your place with him."

He scratched his head. "I'm not sure anymore. I haven't seen him in so long. I just supply the checks, and I don't think Clare even tells him when I send extra for the things he wants." His jaw tightened.

Daniel gripped the steering wheel. "Maybe Clare will marry this guy and you won't have to give her so much money."

He laughed sarcastically. "Fat chance. She won't give up her alimony. Every time I get an increase it goes straight to her." He sighed dejectedly. "Even if I did want to get married again I wouldn't be able to support her."

Daniel pulled into the deserted parking lot and parked the car. "It's quiet here tonight. I thought there'd at least be a few kids hanging around."

Ben glanced around the well-lit parking lot. "Yeah, it is strange. Could be they're being extra cautious with all the murders."

"Well, let's take a look around. Want to check out the bike path first?"

"Okay."

They stepped out of the car and walked toward the edge of the lake. The bright moon cast a romantic glow over the shimmering lake. "It's nice tonight," Daniel said.

"Sure is." Ben pulled a candy bar from his pocket. He tore off the wrapper. "Want half?"

"No, thanks." Daniel scanned the path. "Where the hell is Randy Kane?"

"He could be anywhere," Ben said. "I doubt he's here, though, or we would have seen his bike in the parking lot."

"I suppose you're right, but I don't want to leave any stone unturned."

They walked in silence for a while, shining their flashlights on each side of the path. Ben finished his candy bar, sauntered over to a trashcan, and was ready to toss in the candy wrapper when something on the ground caught his eye. He bent down, picked it up, and held it in the palm of his hand. It was a broken belt buckle. He tossed it into the garbage can along with the candy wrapper. Looking down, he noticed the litter scattered around the can, and it disgusted him. Lazy bastards, he mumbled. He decided to walk over to the picnic tables. As he walked past a few, he noticed some newspapers sticking out from the end of a bench, which faced a wooded area. Rarely did a homeless person sleep here since it was too far from town, but on occasion one could be found, and that's what he assumed he'd find now. He walked over to the bench and gently touched the papers. Just as he'd thought, a soft body was underneath. He'd wake the person up and offer him or her a ride back to town.

"Time to wake up," he said. When he received no response, he removed the papers and shined his flashlight on the person. "Hey, you need to…." He froze at the sight before him. He moved back as the contents of his stomach came up into his throat. He couldn't stop the vomit forcing itself from his body.

CHAPTER TEN

Ben wiped his mouth, walked back over to the body, and shone his light once again on the lifeless form. The head was tilted to the side, but the eyes were open, appearing to stare at him. It was the look in the dead eyes that haunted him. They showed the terror the victim experienced before death claimed him. "Daniel," he called. "I've found something."

"What is it?" Daniel asked, walking quickly to where Ben stood staring down at something on a bench. Ben shined the light on the victim's face.

The color drained from Daniel's face. He swallowed hard as he shined his own flashlight on the rest of the body. "Who could commit such a horrific act?"

Ben shook his head. "We've seen some horrible things on the job, Daniel, but never anything like this."

Daniel choked back the bile rising in his throat. "Most of his left ear has been chopped off." He composed himself the best he could as he examined the rest of the body. "He severed the right leg just below the knee."

"And three fingers are missing from his right hand," Ben

142

observed.

"We need to see if he has any ID," Daniel said slowly. He sucked in his breath and began checking pockets, while trying to avert his eyes from the grisly crime scene.

"You...you think it's Randy Kane, don't you?"

"I hope to God it's not, but who else could it be?" he asked as he pulled a wallet from the boy's back pocket.

Ben stood silently watching as Daniel held the wallet in his hands for a few seconds.

Daniel drew a deep breath, and then flipped the wallet open and shined his light on a boyish face, which stared back at him from a driver's license. He read the name aloud. "Randall Kane." His hand trembled as he looked at his partner. "Two boys from the same family murdered in cold blood. It's senseless, Ben. What could those kids have ever done to deserve such a violent end? These are senseless crimes."

"I don't know, Daniel," Ben said quietly. "He appears to kill just for the thrill of it. We may never know why." He grabbed his phone. "I'll call it in," he said.

Daniel nodded numbly as he fingered the wallet. He dreaded breaking this news to Bill and Mary Kane. And what about Sara? One death in the family was hard enough to cope with, but two in such a short time span was asking way too much for anyone to handle. Especially with the brutal way their lives were snuffed out.

****

Mr. D stood in the shadows waiting for Asher Michaels. He put his hand in his pocket, feeling the smooth handle of the knife. His heartbeat quickened. He loved plunging the knife into a terrified body, watching their eyes as they pleaded with him to let them live. It drenched him with power by giving him total control over his victims. Once the blood started spurting out of them, the feeling of elation was overwhelming.

He hadn't always been this way. In fact, the first time it had happened had been by accident. He'd been remorseful and scared. But as he looked at the man bleeding out in front of him, something changed. He felt invincible. And then he realized that since he had been wronged he had every right to mete out his own form of justice. But something else began to happen, too. He enjoyed killing. He knew he couldn't roam the streets and pick out victims. That would be too risky. But if he could lure people of questionable reputations to work for him, he would actually be able to satisfy his own lust for killing, and at the same time rid the world of these future criminals.

But he would never kill anyone unless they'd wronged him. He knew any of them would if given the chance, since in his business they were responsible for handling large sums of money. Even though he paid them well, the temptation of wanting more would be too hard to resist; they would begin to want more, and then they would take some from the envelopes. At first when they delivered the envelopes to him, he stuffed them into his pocket and sent them on their way. The envelopes were sealed, and he knew that none of his clients would dare stiff him. Why would they want to anyway? They trusted him and he trusted them. If he went down, they'd go along with him.

It wasn't hard to convince a couple of his clients to tell the runners that he'd stiffed them and they were deducting a certain amount. He explained to them that it was a test to see how a new runner would handle the situation. His clients agreed to his test, but most of them were leery about conducting business with someone new. But he assured them that there was no risk to them, and the runners never knew whom they were doing business with in the first place. The runners who could immediately come up with the amount of money the client said was missing were not harmed. They would calmly explain to him what had happened and give him the missing funds, even though they insisted that they'd never taken any of the drugs or money since envelopes were sealed on both ends. In the end, he'd give them a stiff warning and never again would they be on his list of potential victims. The more sordid a runner's past was, the better Mr. D liked it. They were the easy ones. Sometimes he'd let them work for weeks before giving them the test. Other times it might be the second time they went out.

Everything had been running smoothly until he'd hired the Kane boys and they'd asked if their friend Asher Michaels could get a job. There was something about Michaels he didn't like or trust. Especially since he'd brought someone with him to the warehouse. He'd broken one of the most important rules before he'd even gotten the job. He deserved to be punished.

He pulled out a pen flashlight and held it close to his wristwatch. Michaels was already twenty minutes late. Mr. D was pissed. No one ever stood him up. He'd warned him what the consequences would be. He was not a patient man, and as each second ticked by, he felt his blood pressure rise and his anger increase. "Damn him," he muttered. "He'll pay for this." Just like Sara Kane would for talking to the police. He had eyes everywhere.

****

Daniel and Ben knocked on the door. Bill Kane flung the door open, rubbing his swollen eyes. He looked at the detectives expectantly. "Did you find Randy?"

Daniel caught the fear in his eyes. "Can we come in, Bill?"

"Yeah." He led them into the living room. "Do you have

news about Randy?" he anxiously asked again.

"Yes, we do. Can you get your wife?" Daniel asked.

Bill stood shifting his weight from one foot to the other. He swept a hand through his hair. "The doctor gave her some tranquilizers." He took a deep breath.

Daniel placed a hand on the man's shoulder. "I wish I didn't have to tell you this, Bill."

"What?" he asked hoarsely, his eyes darting back and forth. His body trembled.

"There's no easy way to tell you this." He looked sympathetically at him. "We found Randy's body tonight."

"What?" he choked as he sank down on the sofa. "He's dead?" he moaned. "My two boys are dead?"

Daniel watched as the color literally drained from the man's face. He looked like the last bit of air had been sucked out of him.

"How did it happen?"

"He was stabbed several times. We found him near the lake. We believe he was killed in the old warehouse and his body transported to the lake," Ben said gently. "We're sorry for your loss."

"No!" he moaned as he covered his face with his hands. Sobs racked his body, causing him to tremble uncontrollably.

Daniel sat next to him. "Bill, if there's anything I can do for you...I want to help you."

He wiped his face on his shirtsleeve. "Please tell Sara," he sniffed. "I'll break the news to my wife. I don't know what this is going to do to her."

"If you need to talk, please call," Daniel said. "We'll see ourselves out."

He nodded. He sat on the couch, watched the detectives leave, and waited for ten minutes before pulling himself to his feet.

Then with a heavy heart he walked into the bedroom. "Mary," he choked. "Mary, please wake up." He shook her shoulder.

Mary Kane wiped the sleep from her eyes, and then groggily pulled herself to a sitting position. "What's wrong, Bill? Has Randy come home?" She searched his face. "It's more bad news, isn't it?" Her voice was high pitched.

Bill knew his wife didn't want to hear what he had to tell her. It would destroy her. Tears streamed down his face as he gathered her in his arms. "Mary, Randy—"

"I don't want to hear it, Bill," she shrieked, trying to squirm out of his arms. "I want a drink, Bill."

He held her tighter. "You have to listen to me, Mary."

She looked into his red-swollen eyes. "No. Give me a drink first, Bill."

"Mary," he cried. "Both our boys are gone. My God, Mary, we've lost our boys." He held her even closer and sobbed against her chest.

****

Daniel and Ben sat in their car outside the Kane house for a few minutes, trying to deal with their individual emotions.

"Dammit!" Ben said heatedly, slamming his fist on the steering wheel. "It's just not right. Two young lives snuffed out for no apparent reason. What the hell is going on? What the hell did those boys do to deserve to be murdered in such a cold, callous way?"

Daniel shook his head. "I don't know, Ben. It scares me shitless that we have no clue who we're even looking for." He shook his head again. "We've got a sick son-of-a-bitch on our hands, and he's always one step ahead of us."

Ben fumed. "We'll get the bastard. I guarantee it."

Daniel looked hard at him. "We don't even know where

to start, Ben. It could be anybody. We're at a dead end. No one recognizes the composite. Or if they do they're too scared to talk."

Ben exhaled loudly. "I thought the same thing, Daniel. How can we convince someone to talk?"

Daniel exhaled loudly. "We have to keep trying."

Ben frowned. "I don't envy you breaking this news to Sara Kane."

"I wish I didn't have to."

****

Daniel threw his keys on the table, and then removed his shoes. He sat in his easy chair and slowly closed his eyes. He was exhausted, but knew that he couldn't go to sleep. He wished he could block the past few hours from his mind. Randy's lifeless mutilated corpse was transposed on his brain. He would never forget that sight as long as he lived.

He had to tell Sara. How could he possibly find the words to tell her that her other brother was now dead, too, a victim of some fucking monster? The frustration ripping through him made his heart pound erratically. If he could only get his hands on the filthy scumbag. Daniel knew that he could kill the depraved bastard with his bare hands if given the chance. This was the first time in his career that he had ever felt enraged like this, and it scared him. He needed to get his emotions under control.

He popped his eyes open and looked at the mantel clock. 4:45 a.m. He rubbed his eyes, trying to focus. He got up, and then tiptoed upstairs to Taylor's room. He opened the door and peeked inside. Both girls were sleeping soundly. He couldn't wake them. Sara needed all the rest she could get. Later her whole world would be upended once again. He had no idea how she would cope. How would anyone in this situation? He closed the door, and then walked to his own room. He removed his clothes and climbed between the cool sheets.

****

Mr. D dialed Asher Michaels' number. A groggy voice answered on the sixth ring. "I need to speak to Asher," the man demanded.

"Hey listen, buddy, don't you think it's kind of late to be calling someone?" Bob Michaels paused. "Aren't you the same guy who called the other day? You stated you were his employer. I've never heard of a boss calling someone in the middle of the night."

"Are you Asher's father?" Mr. D asked calmly.

"Yes, and I don't appreciate being woken up in the middle of the night."

"I'm sorry, but this is urgent."

"Nothing is so urgent that it can't wait until morning."

"It's in your son's best interest that you get him to the phone now!"

"Has he done something?"

"Let me put it to you this way, Mr. Michaels. I know that your son has had some problems with the law. I'm trying to help him stay out of trouble."

"Hold on," Michaels said after a few seconds. "I'll get him."

The man drummed his fingertips on his dresser as he waited for Asher. His anger was almost uncontrollable. A few minutes later, Asher's voice came over the line.

"Yeah?" Asher asked.

"You didn't show! I warned you that no one double crosses me!"

"Look, I told you that Sara and I aren't seeing each other anymore. I couldn't get her to come with me."

"I told you that I don't like double crossers."

"I didn't double cross you. I haven't even made a delivery for you, so how can you make any accusations against me? And Andy never did anything to you either. He was honest with you."

"Andy betrayed me, as did his brother Randy," Mr. D growled. "No one betrays me and gets away with it."

"What about Randy? He never betrayed you either. Have you heard from him? Everybody's been looking for him."

"They'll find him. In due time. They just haven't looked in the right place." He paused. "Or maybe they have."

"You killed him, too!" he shrieked. "And you want to kill me and Sara!"

The man chuckled. "You can't escape me, son. I'll be watching you and I will get you. That is a promise." He ended the call.

****

"You'll pay for what you did. And you won't get Sara or me. I'll make sure of it." He slammed the phone down, and then realized that Mr. D had already hung up and hadn't heard what he'd said. He sat defeated on the arm of the sofa, wondering what to do. He had no plan to keep Sara safe, or himself for that matter. Perspiration trickled down his back. He shivered. How could he have gotten into such a mess? How could he get out? He didn't know what to do.

Bob Michaels entered the room and walked over to him. He firmly placed a hand on his son's shoulder. "Asher, I want to know what's going on. What sort of trouble are you in?" he demanded. "You've been walking around in a daze the past couple of days. If you've gotten yourself in trouble, you'd better tell me now." Bob stood silently for a few seconds. "Son, I know we've had our rough times, but I want to help you," he said quietly.

Asher turned his head, looked at his father, and saw the worry and concern in his eyes. For the first time in his life, he realized his father really did care about him. He wondered how many sleepless nights he had caused his parents. He'd been a huge part of the reason that had eventually ended their marriage, treating both of them horribly until his mother couldn't take anymore and left. It was a wonder that his father cared anything at all after the way he'd disrespected him. Asher had always done whatever he wanted to do, disregarding any restrictions his father had tried to place on him. He didn't see then that what his father was doing was for his own good. Never once had he considered the pain and suffering his actions were, and had, imposed on him. His father had stood in the shadows, trying his best to help him, and he'd shrugged him off, thinking he had all the answers. Now he needed his father like he'd never needed him before.

"Dad," he choked as a tear slid from his eye, "I'm in a big mess, and I don't know what to do." His shoulders slumped.

"Tell me the problem, Asher. Maybe it isn't as bad as you think it is. We can talk it out. What did you do to cause your boss to call in the middle of the night?"

"Nothing, Dad. I don't know if I can explain it," he sobbed.

"Try, son. Let me help." He squeezed Asher's shoulder.

"Randy and Andy Kane were working for this guy making deliveries…the pay was fantastic. Like it was too good to be true. I begged them to get me a job and they did." He wiped his face on the back of his hand. "Anyway, now Andy and Randy are both dead. Mr. D murdered them."

"What!" His eyes widened. "Was that Mr. D on the phone?"

"Yes," he sniffed.

"How do you know he murdered them?"

"He wanted me to meet him last night and to bring Sara with me. He's going to kill us, Dad," he said in a wobbly voice. "He said he'd get us."

"How do you know for sure he killed the Kane boys? Did he come right out and tell you that he did?"

"Yes." He swallowed hard.

"When did you start working for him?"

"I haven't actually started working yet."

Bob Michaels rubbed his jaw. "You mentioned that Andy and Randy made deliveries. Do you know what the deliveries involve?"

He nodded. "It's running drugs. I'm sorry, Dad." His father looked like the wind had been knocked out of him. Asher felt like shit.

Bob Michaels' shoulders slumped forward. "Are you on drugs, son?" he asked in a low voice. "Please don't lie to me."

"No, Dad. I swear...I never took drugs. I drink beer and sometimes harder stuff, but never drugs." He frowned. "I smoke pot once in a while, but I swear that's it."

"Are you sure the Kane boys are dead? Maybe he's telling you that to scare you."

"I know that Andy's dead. I don't know if Randy is. The police stopped by while you were at work and asked me if I saw him." He swallowed hard. "The last time I saw Randy was when I went with him to make a delivery. The guy shorted him, and he was worried what Mr. D would do if he couldn't come up with the shortage."

"Oh my God!" Bob Michaels covered his face with his hands for a few seconds. "Asher, I can't imagine what you're going through, son." He sat on the sofa and put his arms around him.

"One of my best friends and maybe both are dead," Asher cried, and then broke down sobbing uncontrollably.

After Asher brought himself under control his father spoke. "We're going to have to notify the police, Asher. They'll protect you."

"And Sara?"

"And Sara." He frowned. "What's Sara's connection? Why is he going after her? She wasn't running drugs, was she?"

"No. I brought her with me when I went to talk to him about a job. That's the only connection I can think of." He cleared his throat. "I talked to her earlier, Dad, after I heard about Andy. She was worried because no one can find Randy. I want to help her, but I don't know how."

"You'll help her by seeking justice for the deaths of her brothers when you tell the police everything you know about this Mr. D, and help to put him away for the rest of his life."

Chapter Eleven

Zoey set the phone down. She'd canceled the day's dance classes because her mind was in a fog and she couldn't focus on anything, except telling Daniel and Bella about Hunter and the baby. It had to be done now. The guilt was eating her alive. She quickly left her apartment before she could change her mind.

Thirty minutes later, she was seated in Bella's living room.

"I had Avis make a fresh pot of coffee," Bella said brightly. She picked up the small coffee pot sitting on a tray on the coffee table, and then poured two cups. "We have some of your favorite pastries, too," she said brightly. "Help yourself."

"Thank you. Maybe later," Zoey answered.

Bella scrutinized her. "You look a little peaked. Are you all right?"

Zoey sighed and forced a tight smile. "I'll be fine." She normally would have enjoyed this time chatting with her best friend, but now the weight of the world seemed to be on her shoulders.

"How's everything going with Daniel?"

"I haven't seen much of him, and have barely talked to him

154

for that matter, since I was here for dinner. He's busy with the murder investigation."

Bella sipped her coffee. "We'll all breathe a sigh of relief when that monster is caught."

"It can't be soon enough for me. I get the jitters walking home from the studio."

"Be careful," her friend warned.

"I always am." She looked around the room. "I've always loved this room, Bella. Do you and Hunter intend to live here after the wedding?"

"Yes. Hunter said since I had done such a wonderful job of redecorating, it would be senseless for us to move to another place." She laughed. "He also said that he doesn't have to worry about the ghost of a past husband inhabiting the place."

Zoey leaned forward. "How much do you really know about him?"

"All I need to know. He loves me," she answered defensively. "Lately every time we get together you seem obsessed with Hunter."

"I'm just concerned, that's all."

Bella's eyes narrowed. "Concerned about what?"

"What do you really know about him?"

Bella set down her cup. "Everything I need to, as I already told you. He's involved in many enterprises. I've told you that before. He doesn't have time for regular socializing."

"What about his family? Does he visit them?"

"He's been on his own most of his life and rarely speaks of them. He won't talk about it, but I believe he had a horrible childhood. I don't want to press him and dredge up painful memories for him." She stared at Zoey. "Why the inquisition?" She pursed her lips. "Is there something you know about him that I don't?"

Zoey met her eyes. This was her opening. She drew a long shaky breath and slowly exhaled. "Yes, Bella, there is." In a matter of minutes, both of their lives would forever be altered.

****

Daniel yawned, rubbed his eyes, and glanced at his alarm clock. He got out of bed and pulled on a pair of jeans and a T-shirt. He stretched, then yawned again as he made his way to Taylor's room. The door was slightly open. Daniel peeked into the room, discovering both girls awake and dressed. He hated the task that awaited him, but knew that it couldn't be put off any longer. He lightly knocked on the door.

Taylor turned around. "Hi, Dad. Come on in."

"Good morning, girls." He walked into the room. "Was everything okay last night?"

"Yeah. What time did you get home?" She looked closely at him. "You look awful, Dad!" she exclaimed.

"I was out most of the night. I managed to get a couple of hours of sleep, though." He looked at his daughter and her friend. They both sat on the edge of the bed looking expectantly at him.

"Do you have news about Randy?" Sara asked.

Daniel dreaded the news he was about to deliver. Her question had been tinged with hope. He looked at her pale face. Dark circles were visible under her red-rimmed eyes. "Yes, Sara, I have some news." He stood in the middle of the room, shifting his weight from one foot to the other as he fought for the proper words to deliver the news in the gentlest way he could.

"What is it, Mr. Trevors?" she asked in a trembling voice. "It's not good, is it?"

Daniel lowered his eyes. "I wish there were an easier way to tell you this, Sara."

"What?" she asked fearfully.

He slowly shook his head back and forth. "We found your brother Randy last night."

"Is he okay? Where was he?" she asked.

Daniel's heart broke for her. She was grasping at anything she could, not wanting to hear the truth. "Sara, I wish there was an easier way to tell you," he repeated, shaking his head. "He's dead."

"No!" she screamed, jumping to her feet. "I don't believe you!" She pounded his chest with clenched fists. "No! Please tell me it's not true!"

Daniel grabbed her arms and looked into her grief stricken eyes. "Sara, I'm sorry."

"I can't take this," she moaned. "I don't know what to do."

"Sara, if there's anything Taylor or I can do for you, please tell us."

"What about my parents?" she sobbed. "Do they know?"

"I told your father earlier this morning. I promised him that I would tell you."

"What am I going to do without my brothers?" she cried.

Taylor put her arms around her. "I'm here for you, Sara." Tears streamed down her face. "I'll always be here for you."

Sara sobbed softly. "Thank you," she choked. Her legs wobbled and Taylor helped her back to the bed.

After Taylor had gotten Sara settled back into bed, Daniel motioned to her to follow him into the hall.

Taylor silently closed the door. "Dad, what's going on?" she asked, tears streaming down her face. "Who's going to be next? Why can't the police catch this guy?"

Daniel hugged her like he was afraid to let her go. A part of him was. "Baby, I promise you that we'll get him." He softly brushed the tears from her cheek. "Now I really need you to be strong for Sara. This is going to be the worst time of her life. She needs your strength. Help her, honey. Let her lean on you."

"I'll try, Dad. I just don't know what to say or do for her," she cried.

"You don't have to say or do anything. Sometimes it helps just knowing there is someone who really cares."

She shook her head. "It's like something that happens to other people, but not us." She sniffed. "Nowhere's safe anymore, Dad."

He brushed her hair back from her brow as his gaze penetrated hers. "Honey, we're going to get through this...I promise you."

"I hope so, Dad, but I don't think Sara will ever be the same."

He sighed tiredly. "No, she won't be, but she'll get through it with our love and support."

"I'd better get back to her," Taylor whispered.

Daniel patted her shoulder. "That's a good idea."

"Dad?"

"What, honey?"

"I love you," she said, and then disappeared inside her room.

He walked back into his bedroom, picked up his cell phone, and punched in Zoey's number. Her cheery voice greeted him, and then asked him to leave a message. "It's me, Zoey. I'll call you later," he said, and then clicked off his phone.

****

"Just tell me, Zoey," Bella said tightly. "Has Hunter said something to upset you?"

She slowly let her breath out. "What I'm about to tell you will completely devastate you, but you have to know that I never wanted to hurt you. If I could take it all back I would. I'm so sorry, Bella."

158

Bella leaned forward. "Please stop talking in riddles, Zoey. Just say what you have to. I assume this does have something to do with Hunter."

Zoey twisted her hands together. "Yes. I'm sorry," she said again. She saw the fear come into Bella's eyes.

"What did Hunter say that's upset you?"

Zoey watched the anxiety increase in Bella's eyes. "It's not what he said, it's what he's done."

"Just tell me. Please."

She swallowed hard. "This is difficult for me. You know what our friendship means to me," Zoey said slowly.

"We've been through a lot of difficult times through the years," she agreed. "So please tell me what is going on. For the sake of our friendship."

"It's Hunter," she said in a barely audible voice.

"You've already said that. Quit playing games and tell me what he's done. I'm certain it's probably not as bad as you're making it out to be."

"No. It's worse, Bella." Zoey realized that telling her was even more difficult than she'd thought. It was easy talking to her mirror, but now face to face with Bella was harder than she imagined.

"Enough, Zoey. Just spit it out!" Bella demanded.

"I only wish there was an easier way to tell you." She closed her eyes for a moment, hoping to think of the right words to say, but knew nothing she said would soften the blow she was about to deliver.

"Just tell me, for God's sake," Bella insisted. "The game you're playing is getting old."

Zoey swallowed the lump in her throat. She looked at Bella's pale face, knowing that with the next sentence she would destroy her world, but it was now or never. "Ever since you and Hunter first met, we...we've been having an affair." She lowered her eyes in shame.

Bella's eyes widened and her mouth flew open. She sat for a full minute, staring in disbelief at Zoey. "I don't believe you! How could you do this to me? Why are you trying to destroy my one chance for happiness?" Tears brimmed in her eyes. "Why are you lying, Zoey?" she choked. "Why?"

"I didn't want it to happen," Zoey said remorsefully. "Believe me, Bella, it was not planned." She felt sick to her stomach as shame and guilt overtook her. "I'm sorry," she whispered. "I know that doesn't make up for what I did, but I am so sorry, Bella."

Bella stood and walked to the patio window, looking for a few seconds at the city below. After a few seconds, she whipped around and faced Zoey. "You couldn't stand the fact that a man like Hunter could love someone like me, could you? You've always been the beautiful one with the men falling all over you. But the minute a man shows an interest in me first, your ego can't take it! Your jealousy got the better of you, so you decided to do anything to stop our wedding!" she shrieked. "You must have seduced him." She eyed Zoey coldly. "But then, why should I believe what you're telling me in the first place? You're lying; admit it!"

Zoey shook her head and looked into Bella's cold eyes. She'd never seen that look before, and it frightened her. But everything Bella was saying she deserved. Bella couldn't hurt her any more than she'd hurt herself. In her heart she knew that the friendship she cherished was over. Bella would never forgive her, and she couldn't blame her. "No, I'm telling you the truth. This might sound strange, but I'm trying to protect you. I know I should have come forward sooner, but I couldn't. I was scared. I knew it would destroy our friendship. Please believe me, Bella! He was using you from day one!" she insisted.

"Why do you think I need protection from Hunter?" she smirked. "It doesn't make any sense. It seems like you're the one I need protection from."

"He is only marrying you for the prestige of your name."

"That's the most ridiculous thing I've ever heard," she scoffed.

Zoey realized that no matter what she said Bella would defend Hunter. She'd thought that at least Bella would believe her, but she obviously didn't. Or maybe a part of her didn't want to. "I broke it off with him because I couldn't stand what he was doing to you. I even told him that if he truly wanted me, then to cancel your wedding. But he is only interested in your name. He may have money, but your name opens more doors." She stopped to catch her breath. "Do you really believe I wanted to hurt you?"

Bella began to laugh. "I think you've lost your mind, Zoey. Hunter has been nothing but good to me. He's kind and gentle. If I believed what you're telling me, I have to ask why you would do it. Are you that desperate? Is it because things aren't going as well with Daniel as you'd hoped? My God, you had a wonderful man and you broke his heart. It's a wonder he even gave you another chance. Maybe I should have a talk with Daniel."

Zoey sat quietly to the searing words, but kept silent. There was nothing more she could say. At least not until Bella got everything out of her system.

"Nothing you say would surprise me now," Bella continued. "I'd never know if it was the truth or not. What I can't understand, though, is why you are deliberately trying to destroy my one chance for happiness. I've never met anyone who makes me feel so alive! Without Hunter, I have nothing. None of this means anything to me!" She threw her hands up, making wild gestures at her expensive furnishings. "Money means nothing to me. It can't keep me warm at night. I can't talk to it or make love to it. For the first time in my life I feel truly loved and wanted by a man, but you can't stand it, and for whatever demented reason, you want to destroy it. Do you know how lonely I've been? Do you know how it made me feel to always stand in the background, watching men throw themselves at your feet? I'll never forgive you for this, Zoey. Never! And the funny part is, I have no proof that any of this is true!" she shouted. "I won't destroy what I have with Hunter."

"It is true, Bella. I swear."

"If it is, then the joke is really on me. Then I have to live with the fact that my fiancé has been fucking my best friend!"

"I think he's incapable of loving anyone. If it's any consolation, he doesn't love me either, Bella. He's a narcissist, incapable of loving anyone but himself."

"You don't know that. You don't know him like I do. He's good to me…kind, gentle, and caring. You're a liar!"

"Can't you see what he's doing? That's exactly what he wants you to think. He wants to convince you of his love so as not to arouse your suspicion. At the same time, he's scheming against you. Don't be so damned naïve!"

"Why should I believe you? And what is his scheme? My name? That's ridiculous. He's a self-made man. He certainly is making a name for himself."

"Can you name even one legitimate enterprise he's involved with? I'll bet you can't." Zoey shook her head in disbelief.

"It doesn't matter. He's never asked for a dime from me.

What does it matter how he's earning his money? If it doesn't matter to me, then it sure as hell shouldn't to you!" Bella shouted. "I need to talk to him. I'll get to the bottom of this." She looked disgustedly at Zoey. "I know him well enough to know if he's lying to me. And in this case I will bet my life he's not!"

Zoey sighed heavily. "I know what he's going to tell you. I told him if he didn't leave me alone I was going to tell you about our affair. He said he'd tell you I was lying and was only causing trouble because he had refused my advances." She stood up. "Go see if that isn't what he tells you, Bella."

Bella's eyes flamed. "Just get out!"

"I didn't come here to hurt you. I value our friendship. I know that sounds hypocritical after what I've done, but it's the truth. What I did was horrible and unforgivable. I'll suffer the consequences of it for the rest of my life. It will be your decision as to whom you choose to believe. But right now, I need to talk to Daniel. He'll be hearing what I've just told you." She brushed a tear from her cheek. "One more thing before I go…if you need further proof, Bella, I'm pregnant. A paternity test will prove it. It's Hunter's child I'm carrying, but you'll never know how much I wish it were Daniel's." She walked out of the room, leaving Bella standing in shock.

****

Bob and Asher Michaels walked to the sergeant's desk. "I need to talk to someone right away," he said.

Sergeant Matthews looked up, peering over his glasses at him. "What's the problem?" he asked.

"I have some information about the Kane murders. Threats are being made on my son's life," he anxiously answered as he threw an arm around Asher's trembling shoulders.

The sergeant nodded. "Let me get the detectives handling

the case. You can have a seat in the waiting area."

Asher followed his father to the small room and walked over to the window and looked out at the gray sky. The day matched his mood. He saw no way out of this situation. Asher didn't care about himself, but Sara's life was in jeopardy and he needed to protect her. He ran his hand through his hair. He wasn't just physically exhausted, but mentally exhausted, too, and didn't know which was worse. His two best friends were dead. That hadn't sunk in all the way yet. Asher knew that the finality of their deaths would hit him soon, and he would have to deal with it, but he didn't know how he could go on without the only true friends he'd ever had. His heart squeezed. They were Sara's brothers, and he couldn't even comprehend her loss. He vowed to protect and help her in any way he could. He glanced at his father.

Bob Michaels sat in a metal folding chair. He sighed tiredly. Asher knew he hadn't been able to get back to sleep after Asher had confided in him.

****

Bob Michaels felt like a zombie. He was going through the motions, but couldn't comprehend the severity of the situation. He was frozen in fear and his only concern was to help his son. If only Asher hadn't allowed himself to be caught up in this mess. Michaels blamed himself. He wasn't home much, but when he was, they barely spoke more than a few words to each other. He vowed that was going to change. Asher and he hadn't gotten along for a long time, and now Asher needed him like he'd never needed him before. Bob sat back in the metal chair and looked at his son.

He remembered when Asher was just an infant and he had walked the floors with him, sharing his own hopes and dreams with his baby boy. He had bonded with his son from the very moment he'd laid eyes on him and had believed they would always have a special closeness, and they had. But when Asher hit his teenage years things started to change. His values and morals revolved around his own concept of what was right or wrong. The only opinion that seemed to matter to him was his own. Asher didn't care who he hurt with his rudeness and ruthless behavior. Bob stood by, watching his son slowly turn into a stranger, someone he almost didn't recognize any more.

When he'd tried to reach out to Asher, the boy only rebelled further. He tried everything to bring back the son he'd once known. Showering him with gifts and money only made Asher want more, and nothing satisfied him for long. It hadn't taken Bob long to realize this. He knew deep in his heart that Asher's behavior was one of the reasons his wife had chosen to pack up and depart two years ago, leaving behind her husband and wayward son. She had reached the end of her rope. It wasn't until Ruthie had left that he realized the stress she'd been under. Towards the end of their marriage it had turned into a power play between mother and son, and Asher was always the victor. How many times had she begged Bob to see what overindulging Asher was doing to them?

Bob blinked his tired eyes. In the end, he had lost his wife. She hadn't even requested custody, but told her lawyer that she could not raise Asher. A year later Bob pleaded with her to come back, but she refused. For her own sanity, she needed to stay away. Unless she saw a radical change, she wouldn't even visit. She had only been to the house a few times, and Bob had taken her to dinner several times, but she made no attempt at reconciliation. He wondered if this would change her mind. He was certain that Asher was changed. Maybe this would bring

Ruth back to him and their son. Asher needed his mother, even though he'd refused to see her or even talk to her.

"Mr. Michaels, we understand that you have some information about the Kane murders." Daniel said, hurrying over to him with a folder in one hand.

"Yes, my son does." He pointed to Asher.

Asher walked over to them.

"We've met," Daniel said, looking at the teenager.

Bob Michaels frowned. "You have?"

"We came by the other day to question your son about Randy Kane."

"I was trying to get a job with Andy and Randy," he said slowly, watching Ben Wilson walking towards them. "I told you that."

"Yes, you did," Daniel answered.

"I've got a conference room," Ben said to Daniel.

"Thanks. Let's go down the hall." They walked in silence to the room. Daniel held the door open until everyone was inside, and then closed the door. They seated themselves around a conference table.

Daniel observed the boy's red-rimmed eyes. "I understand that you called my home last night to talk to Sara Kane?"

He nodded. "Yes, Mr. D wanted me to bring Sara to the old train depot, because the police would be watching the warehouse. The warehouse was where Andy and Randy made the drops. That's where I met Mr. D to ask him for a job."

"Before we get into this, can I get anyone some coffee, juice, or a soda?" Ben asked. They declined and he seated himself.

"Did you meet Randy and Andy through their sister?" Daniel asked, eyeing Asher.

Asher folded his hands and rested them on the table. "Yes."

166

"What type of work did they do?"

"They exchanged envelopes and brought the proceeds to Mr. D at the warehouse every night. The reason I wanted a job was because they made good money."

"Does Mr. D have another name?" Daniel asked.

Asher shrugged his shoulders. "That's all I know him by. That's what Randy and Andy called him, too."

"Do you know where he lives?"

"No, but it's probably somewhere nice because he dresses like he's rich." His forehead furrowed. "I guess he is rich since he can pay so much."

"What kind of car does he drive?"

"I don't know. He was always at the warehouse and I never saw a car."

"Was he always there before his employees arrived with the envelopes?"

"I don't know. I only went a couple of times. He was there first, then."

"Did you boys ever wonder what was in the envelopes?"

"We aren't stupid," Asher answered defensively, "but the money was too good to care. That's why I begged Randy and Andy to get me a job, too. I wasn't working for him yet, but sometimes would go with Randy and Andy. But not when they went to deliver the envelopes to Mr. D except for those couple of times."

"Why not?" Daniel asked.

Asher fidgeted in his chair. "I wasn't even supposed to go with them at all. Mr. D got pissed those couple of times I went to drop the envelopes with them. He would have gone off if he knew I was meeting the clients with them, too."

"You obviously knew that Randy and Andy Kane were drug

runners, didn't you?" Ben asked, taking over the questioning.

"Not at first. Most of the people Andy and Randy dealt with looked like ordinary businessmen."

"Was anyone else ever with Mr. D at the warehouse?"

"No. He was always alone."

"Can we cut to the chase here?" Bob Michaels asked. "My son's life has been threatened. If he's the serial killer we've been hearing about, then I think we need to focus on keeping my son safe."

"I understand your concern, Mr. Michaels. We're trying to get some background. We have every intention of providing protection to your son due to the circumstances," Daniel assured him.

Bob Michaels relaxed. "Thank you," he answered, relieved.

Ben studied Asher. "Did he say why he wanted you to bring Sara to him last night?"

"To kill us," he answered matter-of-factly.

Daniel looked up in surprise. "Did he say those exact words?"

Asher's face paled. "He said if I didn't bring Sara to him that I would be sorry. He said he would find us." He swallowed hard. "He already told me that he killed Randy and Andy, so why would I doubt that Sara and me wouldn't be his next victims?" He twisted his hands together.

"Why does he want to kill Sara?" Ben questioned.

"Because she can describe him. She went with me one night when I was meeting him about the job. I told her not to come up to the warehouse and to stay with the bike, but I think she got scared in the dark and came looking for me. She kept herself hidden, but he must have somehow seen her or followed after me when I met her on the path."

"Do you know if the Kane boys ever met him at the old train

depot?"

He shook his head. "I don't know."

"Can you give us a description of Mr. D?" Daniel asked.

"Like I said, he always wears expensive clothes." He frowned. "He's maybe my dad's age, kind of muscular. He looks like he works out a lot. He must be intelligent."

"Why do you think that?" Ben asked.

"It's just the way he talks. Very proper."

"Does he have any tattoos or noticeable scars?"

"No, nothing I saw. But then again, it was always dark." He looked at the detectives. "Look, you've got to catch him! I don't care about myself, but I won't let him hurt Sara! It doesn't matter where she is, he has a way of finding people."

"We won't let him hurt either of you," Daniel replied. "I have an alarm system at my house. Sara's safe there."

"He'll find a way. Believe me. I think he likes killing. He doesn't even feel bad about it. You've got to help her before it's too late!"

"Calm down, Asher. Sara's safe," Daniel answered. "I'll send a patrol car over there to check everything out."

"Good."

Ben set the composite in front of Asher. "Is this him? Is this Mr. D?"

Asher's eyes grew wide with fear. "That's him! That's Mr. D!" His hands shook as he held the picture.

****

Hunter wiped the steam from the mirror, and twisted his body this way and that to better admire himself. His cell phone buzzed, interrupting him.

"Hello," he snapped.

"Hunter, it's me," Bella said tonelessly.

169

"I'm sorry I answered so brusquely, honey," he apologized. He grabbed a towel off the towel rack and wrapped it around his waist. "What's up?"

"We need to talk as soon as possible."

He instantly picked up on the serious tone of her voice. He wasn't in the mood for any negativity. Everything was running smoothly, and he didn't want anyone or anything to spoil his euphoric mood. He rolled his eyes and pretended to care about whatever was bothering her this time. "Is something wrong? Do we have a problem with the wedding plans? Later I'll be free to help, but right now I need to take care of some loose ends with one of my investments. In fact, I'm in the middle of a meeting right now," he lied.

"It has nothing to do with the wedding plans, Hunter. I don't give a damn if you're in a meeting. You need to listen to me. I received a visit from someone, and it has left me quite upset."

"Whom?"

"I don't want to go into it over the phone. Just get here as soon as possible. I really need to talk to you, Hunter."

"Okay, honey. I'll be over early this afternoon. Don't be upset. Whatever someone said to upset you, I'll take care of."

"Just get here as soon as you can," she insisted.

CHAPTER TWELVE

The man stood, looking curiously at the house. It looked like something out of a magazine, he thought. Quaint, but comfy, with a well-manicured lawn and flowers bordering either side of the walk. A white picket fence encircled the lawn. One hundred percent Americana, right out of the fifties, he thought, amused.

He cautiously looked around himself. Seeing no one on the street, he walked over to the garage and peered inside a side window. It was empty, just as he had hoped it would be. The man tried the door, then laughed when he found it unlocked. Even if it had been locked, the cheap lock would have been a cinch to pick. He sneaked inside, closed the door, then pulled a blond wig from his pocket and quickly put it on. He had a vast collection of wigs in various styles and hair colors, along with an assortment of eyeglasses and mustaches. There would be no need to worry about his voice being recognized, since she'd never heard him speak. Today he'd opted for an inexpensive suit, not his usual expensive tailor mades. The man had also decided not to wear a mustache, but would wear a pair of eyeglasses. He chose a tinted pair. There was no way he'd be recognized. Smiling, he took a small mirror from the breast pocket of his suit coat and examined his image. He was satisfied with the result and snapped the mirror case shut, then placed it back into his pocket.

The man opened the door slightly, and seeing it was clear, hurried out of the garage and to the sidewalk in front of the house. Casually walking to the front door, he smoothed his breast pocket and then rang the doorbell. When he received no response, he rang the bell a second time.

Taylor breathlessly flung the door open. "If you're selling something, we're not interested." She started to close the door.

He put a hand on the door, preventing her from closing it. "No, I'm not a salesman. I'm here to see Sara Kane," he said. "Her parents sent me. They have requested that she pick out the headstones for her brothers' graves since the three of them were so close." His voice was low and solemn.

Taylor looked at him suspiciously. "I don't know. Sara didn't mention anything about that to me."

"I'm sorry. I should introduce myself. My name is Stan Lupas from Drake Memorials. I've been asked to pick Miss Kane up to drive her downtown to look at our selection of headstones."

Taylor frowned as she hesitated for a minute. "Hold on and I'll go ask her." She closed the door. A few minutes later, she returned with Sara.

"I'm Sara Kane." Sara stared at him. "You're here about headstones for my brothers?"

"Yes." He looked at her red puffy eyes. "May I offer you my deepest condolences on the loss of your brothers," he said softly, at the same time gently taking her hand.

"Thank you," she whispered.

"Has your friend explained to you why I'm here?" He was shocked by the young girl's beauty now that he saw her close-up.

Her slender frame was clothed in a pair of baggy blue jeans and a dark blue sweatshirt, but still her delicate beauty showed through. Her long black hair was drawn back in a ponytail, lending a rare view of her high cheekbones. His heartbeat quickened when he looked into her coal-black eyes. Her full, pink lips were drawn up as she looked questionably at him.

"Yes."

"Shall we be on our way, then?" he politely asked. "I've picked out some beautiful stones to show you, any of which will be a real tribute to your brothers."

"My parents haven't made any funeral arrangements as far as I know." She looked apprehensively at him, then at Taylor as she rubbed the back of her neck. "Taylor, I don't know what I should do."

Taylor grabbed her arm. "We'd better wait for my dad, Sara," she answered, nervously eyeing the stranger. "He'll be here in a few minutes. Let's see what he says."

The man glanced at his wristwatch. "I can't wait. I have several other appointments this morning." He lifted an eyebrow as he peered at Sara. "We need to pick out the headstones now. If you wait too long, your brothers won't have a marker for their graves. The choice is yours."

Sara's eyebrows knitted together. "I don't even know when their funerals are," she replied suspiciously.

"Soon, from what I've been told," he answered. He glanced at his wristwatch again.

Sara looked at Taylor. "What do you think? I don't know what to do. Maybe I should go. I don't want my brothers in unmarked graves."

"I'd wait," Taylor cautioned. "At least until you talk to your parents or my Dad. Something doesn't sound right. I'm sure your parents would have called and told you." She glared at the stranger. "I think you'd better go."

The man knew he had to think of something fast. "Your parents will be disappointed. I'm sure you don't wish to burden them any more than they already are. They are only trying to help you with your pain, Sara." He sighed. "But, as I said, it's your decision. I'll have to inform your parents that you wouldn't go." He turned to leave.

"Wait!" Taylor called. "Why didn't they pick them out themselves, or at least take Sara with them?"

Good, a change of heart. Inside he was elated, but had to maintain his professional decorum. He stopped, and then turned smoothly on his heel as he answered her. He looked directly into Taylor's eyes. "It is their wish that Sara do this, as she was very close to them. They thought it a fitting tribute to them from her."

"I don't know," Taylor answered, still suspicious. She looked at Sara. "I still think you should wait until my father gets here, or call your parents."

Sara sighed. "No. I'll go. I have to do it for my brothers." She looked at the stranger. "But can you drive me back here afterwards?"

"Of course. I'll have you back in an hour. That's if we leave right now."

"Okay, then." She hugged Taylor goodbye. "Tell your dad where I'll be."

"I don't think you should go, Sara. Please wait for my dad," Taylor cautioned.

Sara's eyes pleaded with her. "I have to do this for my brothers. Please understand."

"Where's your cell phone?" Taylor asked.

"In the bedroom charging. I haven't charged it for a couple

of days and it died."

"Maybe that's why your parents haven't called you," Taylor reasoned.

"They would have called your landline. You know, how I always do when I forget my phone."

"I still don't think you should go if you're not going to have your cell phone. How will I reach you?"

"She'll be back before you know it," the man replied.

"It'll be okay," Sara assured her. "I'll probably be back before your father even gets here."

****

Taylor watched as Sara and the man made their way down the walk. She wondered why his car wasn't parked at the curb out front. They walked to the corner, then turned out of sight. She slowly closed the door. This didn't feel right. She wished she could have persuaded Sara not to go. An uneasy feeling came over her and a chill ran up her spine. The man was creepy. But then, she thought, why wouldn't he be? He worked at a funeral home.

****

Sara walked in silence next to the tall man. Something about him seemed familiar, but she was certain she had never seen him before. She stole a glance at him. She couldn't place him, but the feeling that she somehow knew him wouldn't leave her.

"I'm sorry I parked so far from the house," he apologized, "but I wasn't sure of the address, and with it being such a nice day, I figured a little exercise wouldn't hurt since I spend so much of my time indoors due to my work." He laughed. "Nowadays with computers, video games, and everything else electronic, you teens don't get out into the fresh air much anymore. No, you kids today stay stuck inside while the beauty of nature is right

175

outside your door. Instead of socializing face to face, you would rather text and socialize through all the networking sites."

Sara was offended by his remarks, but wasn't in the mood to argue with him. Any other time she would have, but not today. She was drained. She remained silent, but she wished he would quit talking. Maybe he didn't realize it, but he definitely was making her feel worse. Her brothers were dead, her whole world was turned upside down, and all this asshole could do was talk about things he knew nothing about. She doubted he had kids, but if he did, she certainly felt sorry for them.

"Here we are," he announced as they approached a dark blue medium sized sedan. He held the door for her, and then closed it after she was safely inside. He quickly made his way to the driver's side and slid behind the wheel, then started the car and proceeded down the street.

He stole several glances at her, which made Sara very uncomfortable. She pretended that she didn't see. She just wanted to pick out the stones and get back to Taylor's house.

"How old are you?" he asked.

"Fourteen," she answered quietly.

"You look much older," he observed.

She didn't respond. She still had a nagging feeling that she knew him from somewhere, and she wished she could remember.

"Do you have a boyfriend?"

"No," she answered, thinking his question too personal. Now her discomfort was mounting.

"I'm surprised boys aren't beating a path to your door," he said softly.

Sara's guard went up. That was an odd thing for him to say. "Hardly. I had a boyfriend, but we broke up."

"I'm sorry," he said sympathetically. "Especially with your

present situation. You could certainly use his support." He paused. "What's his name?"

"Why?" She looked skeptically at him.

"No reason." He smiled faintly. "I'm just trying to make small talk. I'm sorry if I said anything to offend you."

Sara wondered if his oddness was because he spent so much time with dead people that he didn't know how to act with real live humans. She decided to cut him a little slack, even though he still gave her the creeps. "No, you didn't. His name is Asher Michaels." She looked at the scenery whizzing by. "Maybe we'll work things out. We're talking."

"That's good. The name doesn't ring a bell. Is he new in town?"

"No. He's lived here all of his life."

"I see." He stopped talking and began to hum a popular tune as they continued their drive.

Sara rested her head on the plush headrest. She closed her eyes for a few minutes, listening to the traffic. When she opened her eyes again, she noticed that they were several miles out of the city. She bolted upright in her seat. "Where are we going?" she asked, alarmed.

The man smiled. He grabbed her hand. "Don't you remember me?" he asked.

She pulled her hand away. "Should I? I never met you before today," she said uneasily, now realizing her instincts were right about his familiarity.

"Think real hard now, Sara," he prompted. "It'll come to you."

She racked her mind, but still could not place him. She clasped her hands together and swallowed hard as fear began to overtake her. "Please take me back to Taylor's. Her dad's a cop, you know,

177

and when he finds out I've gone with you, they'll have the whole force out looking for me. I shouldn't have come."

He laughed. "That's highly unlikely that anyone will be looking for you. Do you really think you matter that much to anyone?" He pulled one of her hands free and squeezed it. "Are you certain you don't remember me? Because I certainly remember you." He grinned.

"No! I don't know who you are. Look, just let me out and I'll get a ride back." Sara was choked with fear. "Please let me go!" she shrieked.

"Think about where you've met me," he prodded. "Come on. Try." His eyes narrowed. "Or maybe you do remember and are afraid to tell me."

"Look, I don't know you. You must have me mixed up with someone else. Let me go and I won't tell anyone about this," she bargained. "I promise."

"Come on," he insisted. "Even though we never *actually* met, you did see me," he snarled as he reached over, opened the glove box, and took out a black mustache and black wig. He removed the blond wig and placed the black one in its place. He glanced in the mirror, adjusting the wig as he kept one hand on the steering wheel. Next, he put on the black mustache. "Remember now?"

She screamed, clutching the door handle and trying to open it.

He chuckled. "Sorry. It won't do you any good…automatic lock." He reached for her again, placing a warm hand on her arm. "I don't want to hurt you, Sara." She shrugged his hand off. "So, you and Michaels broke up. Wasn't man enough for you, huh?"

"What do you want from me?" she cried.

"Now what do you think?" he taunted.

"I don't know!"

"You saw me when your lover boy stopped by one night."

"So." She avoided his penetrating eyes. "All I know is you were supposed to give him a job."

"Don't play games with me!" His voice became harsh. "You talked to the police and gave them a description of me." He snickered as he turned his head and glared at her. "But the sad part for you is that that person in the composite doesn't exist. If I could fool you, then I can fool anyone."

"Then why are you doing this to me? I didn't do anything to you."

He sighed. "That's a matter of opinion. You know that I killed your brothers. No one *ever* double-crosses me! They found that out the hard way. I can't let you live after you went to the police."

Tears streamed down her face. "You are evil! I hope you burn in hell!" she cried.

He laughed as he maneuvered the car down a dark, wooded road. "Don't worry...I won't harm you. I'll wait so your boyfriend can watch you die!" he snarled.

Sara stared at him with terror stricken eyes. "You're going to kill him, too" she choked.

****

Daniel raced into the house. "Taylor!" he called.

"In here, Dad," she answered.

He tore into the kitchen, raced over to her, and then embraced her.

She set down the glass she'd been rinsing. "Dad, what's wrong? You're hugging me like I'm going to disappear or something."

"Thank God you're all right," he said, squeezing her close. He glanced around the kitchen. "Where's Sara?" He released his hold on her.

179

Taylor wiped her hands on a dishtowel. "Some guy came to pick her up. Her parents sent him so she could pick out headstones for Randy and Andy. She said she'd be back in an hour, so she should be here any time now. I didn't want her to go 'cause the guy was weird, but she said it'd be okay."

"Well, as long as her parents sent him, I suppose it's all right." He sat down. "Honey, we've got some information about the murders."

"Do you know who the guy is?" she asked hopefully.

"No, not yet, but he did admit to it. He's also made threats on Sara's and Asher Michaels' lives."

Her eyes grew wide with fear. "Why, Dad? What did they do?"

"Sara apparently can identify him. We're having police protection for the Kanes, the Michaels, and our home."

"Do you really think he would do something to Sara and Asher?" she asked, trembling.

He shook his head. "I don't know, honey. He's already killed, so I wouldn't put anything past him." He looked at his daughter's pained face. "Taylor, I don't want to scare you, but you have to be extremely careful. Don't let your guard down for one minute. I don't want you to answer the door for anyone when I'm not here. And I want the security on at all times. Promise me."

"I promise, Dad."

"I've got to go out for a little while. Call my cell when Sara gets back to let me know she's home."

****

Thirty minutes later Daniel stood in the center of Zoey's living room. By the expression on her face, she was deeply distressed about something. She was pale and drawn, quite the contrast to her normally vibrant self. "Are you sick, Zoey?" he asked.

She shook her head. "No." She inhaled deeply. "This is going to be one of the most difficult things I've ever had to do." She tenderly touched his cheek. "You are such a sweet, gentle man, Daniel. And I sincerely do love you with all my heart. Always remember that." Tears filled her eyes. "I'm sorry for ever hurting you."

"I know. I never stopped loving you, Zoey. I just need time. We've been over this."

"To see if you'll ever be able to trust me again," she said.

He rubbed his jaw. "Let's not get into that right now. I want to know why you're upset. Has something happened?"

She sank down onto the sofa. "Just hold me, Daniel."

He sat next to her and held her close. "What's wrong, Zoey? Please, let me help." He turned her head until she was facing him. His eyes bore into hers. Never before had he seen so much pain in someone's eyes. Her news had to be devastating, so he braced himself for whatever it was.

"Daniel, I love you more than anything in this world." Her voice was gentle.

"I love you, too," he whispered as he watched her fight back tears.

She cleared her throat. "I know you're exhausted from the murder investigation, but this can't wait any longer."

"I'm sorry I haven't been around much, and I have to get back in a little while, but I want you to know that you're important to me, too, Zoey."

"I hope so," she whispered. "But I'll understand if you never want to see me again."

"Nothing can be so bad that I wouldn't want to see you," he said softly, enclosing her small hand in his.

She swallowed hard. "I'm going to try to explain this the best

181

that I can. But, please, always remember how much I love you and always will," she said as her voice cracked.

"I'm listening." He squeezed her hand. "Nothing can be worse than what we've already been through," he assured her.

"This is."

Daniel braced himself. He didn't think anything could be worse than when she'd broken his heart.

"Earlier today I had this same conversation with Bella." She cleared her throat. "She's going to have to make one of the hardest decisions of her life. I only pray that she makes the right one. Maybe someday she will also find it in her heart to forgive me."

He frowned. "Bella is your best friend."

She shook her head. "Not anymore, as far as she's concerned."

He frowned again. "Now I'm really in the dark. What could you have possibly done that would affect both Bella and me? Just tell me what's going on, Zoey."

"Daniel, please believe me when I tell you that I never wanted to hurt you. But I can't live with this dishonesty hanging between us."

"What dishonesty?"

"I haven't been totally honest with you."

He stiffened. "You've been lying to me?" The softness left his voice.

She nodded. "When Hunter Tucker and Bella first met, I knew that he was attracted to me. He's been using Bella." She drew a shaky breath. "Shortly after they met, Hunter and I began an affair." She looked at him.

Daniel's facial muscles tensed. "So, you were sleeping with him while you and I were together?" he hoarsely asked. "Is that what you're telling me?" His worst suspicions were coming true.

He didn't want to believe it.

She lowered her eyes.

"Dammit, Zoey, answer me!" Even though he knew the truth, he needed to hear her say it, but she wouldn't even meet his eyes.

"Yes," she whispered without looking at him.

He was silent for a few seconds as her admission crashed into his brain. When he finally spoke, he chose his words carefully. "Was Hunter the reason you broke off with me?"

She swept a shaky hand through her hair. "Yes. I was mixed up. I really thought I loved him and he loved me back." She blinked hard. "But I was so wrong. He was using me, too. It took us breaking up to realize that it's been you I've loved all along, not Hunter."

Daniel put his head in his hands. His shoulders heaved up and down as his soul slowly became crushed under the weight of her words. She'd hurt him like he'd never been hurt before. It was over. For good this time. No more chances. He could never trust her again. But he needed answers. After a few minutes, he raised his head, and with tears streaming down his face asked, "When we got back together, was it because you wanted me, or did you have another reason?"

She touched his shoulder as her own tears fell. "Daniel, I always cared for you. It was you all along I truly loved. I was confused. Hunter was only an infatuation."

"That wasn't my question, Zoey," he said weakly.

"I wanted to break off with Hunter. He wouldn't let me, so I thought if he believed you and I had gotten back together he would leave me alone."

"So no matter what you say about loving me and needing me, the truth is that you were only using me to end your affair with Hunter," he said hoarsely.

183

"No, no," she emphatically replied. "This is coming out all wrong. I can explain."

"When did you end the affair?"

"When you and I got back together. That's the truth, Daniel," she sobbed. "I swear. I haven't been with Hunter since we got back together."

He exhaled loudly. "So, let me get this straight. You didn't get back with me because you loved me, needed me, or even wanted me. It was to make Hunter leave you alone."

"No, Daniel! Listen to me! I always did care about you."

"Loving someone and caring about someone aren't always the same thing." He blinked hard.

"I did fall in love with you...a long time ago. I was only too blind to see it. It was always there, buried deep within my heart." Tears splashed down her cheeks. "It's always been you, Daniel."

He shook his head in disbelief. "No. It comes back around to the fact that you used me. It was convenient to rekindle our relationship to keep Hunter at bay." His voice cracked. "There's really nothing more to say, Zoey." He looked at her. "I'm sorry I gave you a second chance. We're done for good this time."

"No, please don't say that! We can work it out. Just give me a chance to make it up to you."

Daniel looked at her in disbelief. "Do you hear yourself, Zoey? Put yourself in my place. What would you do?"

"I would forgive you."

"No. I don't believe you would."

Tears splashed down her face. "I love you so much, Daniel. Why won't you believe that? You're the reason I broke off with Hunter. It's been you all along. I've only wanted you."

"That's why you cheated. Because you love me." He was drained. "Just don't say anything more, Zoey. I've heard enough." He rubbed the back of his neck. "I've got to go." He headed toward the door.

"You don't know how I've suffered with this betrayal, Daniel," she called after him. "I've hurt the two people I care most about. You and Bella. I don't blame you if you never want to see me again. But I will always love you, Daniel. Please believe that."

He stopped and turned to face her. "I don't blame Bella for ending her friendship with you."

"I don't either, and I can only pray that someday she'll find it in her heart to forgive me and maybe we can be friends again."

"Quit playing victim, Zoey. It's getting old." He rubbed his eyes, wishing the pain would go away, but it wouldn't. His chest was heavy. Heavy from the burden of his heart slowly shattering and breaking into a thousand little pieces. "I loved you so much," he said, choking on his tears.

She touched his arm. "We can work through this. This can make us stronger."

A tear escaped from his eye and began a slow decent down his cheek. "No. Never again," he vowed.

"I never wanted to hurt you. Please believe me. Our love can overcome this," Zoey said in a shaky voice. "Just give us a chance!"

"How would I ever know if you're telling me the truth? How do I know if you're hiding something else?"

"There is one more thing." She lowered her eyes. "I'm pregnant."

He was stunned. If it was his, he would do right by his child. "Is it mine?"

She met his eyes and then slowly shook her head.

"Damn you!" he cried. "Damn you!" He opened the door

and walked out of the apartment.

CHAPTER THIRTEEN

Sara was frozen with fear. All she could see was sunlight filtering through a rotted wall in the dark musty shack. Where was she? She tried to move her wrists and ankles, but it was no use. They were tightly bound. Even if she hadn't been tied up, where would she go? She was in the middle of nowhere, and the nearest house was miles away. He hadn't brought her to the warehouse. That's where she assumed he'd take her, but then again, that would probably be the first place the police would look. Sara had thought he was going to kill her when they arrived, but she remembered that he said he wanted Asher to see her die. He'd silently taken some rope from a large shoulder bag, secured her wrists and ankles, and then left. When would he return? She cried until she was all cried out, but now she had to think. She could scream, but no one would hear her. Her cries for help would only fall on deaf ears. Sara had to conserve her energy and try to overcome her fear and think rationally. But that was easier said than done. He would kill her eventually. He'd killed her brothers, and now he was going to kill Asher and her. That must be where he went…to get Asher. She prayed that he wouldn't get to him. If he tried, maybe by then the police would catch him. If they did, would he tell them where she was? No. He was evil. He'd let her die a slow painful death all alone out here. Maybe no one would ever find her body. Death awaited her either way, and there was nothing she could do about it.

Her paternal grandmother's image suddenly popped into her mind. Sara and her brothers had been close to her. They could count on her for the love and security their parents didn't offer. She'd been dead for a few years now, the victim of a painful cancer; but conversations they had shared from the past filtered through her mind now, like a book left open by a window with a gentle breeze slowly lifting and turning the pages.

These were the pages of her short life. There were so many things she'd never get to do, so many places she'd never see. She closed her eyes and concentrated on her grandmother, letting her spirit course through her body. It filled her with a sense of peace she didn't understand. Maybe this was the peace her grandmother had told her about. When her grandmother was nearing the end of her life, she spoke freely about death. Her face would light up when she talked about the dearly departed family members she would soon be joining. Sara had been fascinated, wondering what it would feel like. She wanted to know why most people feared something they could never escape. Grandmother had embraced death with open arms. Had her brothers found that same peace at the end of their lives?

Her eyes popped open and the peacefulness slowly left her, replaced by the urgent need to fight for her life.

****

Daniel parked his car in a secluded spot in a parking lot near the park. He needed to think. He was shattered. He didn't know what hurt worse...Zoey's betrayal, or the fact that he had let

188

himself be used. His emotions were jumbled. He ran his hand over the stubble on his chin. His heart was ripped wide open and he couldn't stop the bleeding. Maybe he never would.

He rested his head on the steering wheel, letting his mind go where it chose. He had no control over his thoughts. Zoey had said when she'd dumped him that she just wanted to be friends. He scoffed. But she'd lied. She'd been screwing her best friend's fiancé while she was still with Daniel. What a fool he'd been to give her a second chance. No wonder she'd pushed him into getting back together and wanting to be married. She wanted him to father her lover's baby. Well, at least she'd told him that. What if she hadn't and he had married her? Would she have kept that dirty little secret, letting him believe he was the baby's father?

He sighed dejectedly. He wanted to be past this hurt, this heart wrenching pain. He bit his bottom lip, trying to suppress all the emotions begging to be released. His head throbbed. He was hurt, angry, and emotionally exhausted.

"Damn you!" he yelled as he pounded the steering wheel with a clenched fist. He didn't know how to get past this pain. Had she really expected that he could just forget this and pick up where they had left off? Knowing that she was at this moment carrying another man's child inside of her? Did she think he was a fool? It would take a long time for his fragile heart to heal, if ever. Tears brimmed in his eyes. He cried for the love he and Zoey had once shared. How could she have thrown it away? He had treasured their time together and the plans they had made. In time he knew he would have married her. He'd loved her deeply, and the strange thing was that no matter how badly she'd betrayed him, he still did. God help him for loving a woman who'd just ripped his heart out with her bare hands. Why couldn't he hate her? His lips trembled as his hot heavy tears fell.

****

Asher paced the living room floor. Every few seconds he looked out the window at the unmarked police car parked across the street.

"Son, let me get you something to eat," Bob Michaels said, laying a strong hand on his son's shoulder.

He shook his head. "No thanks, Dad. I'm not hungry."

"You've got to eat, Asher," his father prompted. "You need to keep up your strength."

"The thought of food makes me sick to my stomach." He searched his father's face. "Dad, I've really messed up bad this time. No matter what anybody says, I only have myself to blame. It's bad enough what I did to myself, but Sara shouldn't have to suffer." He clenched and then unclenched his fists. "Dad, I really hurt her. She never did anything wrong. I wanted to prove what a big man I was. Yeah, some big man I turned out to be! When this is over, Dad, I promise I'll make you proud of me; no matter what it takes."

Bob Michaels pulled him close. "You already make me proud, Asher. Admitting your mistakes and really wanting to change is what makes a real man, son, and you've already admitted your faults and have changed by doing that."

Asher's cell phone buzzed. He didn't recognize the number. He looked at his father. "It's got to be him. He warned me that I'd better answer my cell."

"Go ahead," his father urged.

Asher pressed a button. The familiar but dreaded voice came over the line. Asher tightened his grip on the phone as the color drained from his face and his throat dried out.

"I want you to meet me, Michaels. The game is over. It's time," Mr. D said.

Bob Michaels laid a hand on Asher's shoulder.

His father's support filled him with confidence. He smirked. "Are you crazy? I'm not meeting you, now or ever. You can't hurt me."

"Really? Who do you think is going to help you? The police?" He laughed shrilly. "They can't be everywhere."

"You won't get away with killing all those people."

"I already have. Now shut up and listen to me, punk! And you'd better listen very carefully if you ever want to see your girlfriend again. I've got Sara."

"I don't believe you." Asher stuffed a hand into his pocket. "Sara is safe."

The man laughed. "You'd better believe me when I tell you that she's not safe, but with me right now."

"Prove it," Asher taunted, knowing Mr. D was trying to call his bluff.

"I don't have to prove anything to you, but if you have a brain, you'll listen to what I have to say. Sara *is* with me. No one will ever find her. She's safely tucked away. I'm giving you the opportunity to say goodbye to her tonight. Either way she's going to die."

"You're lying! You think I'm stupid?"

"Yes, I do think you are stupid, but that's beside the point. Once I hang up, your chance to say goodbye is over. Oh, by the way, in case you don't believe what I'm telling you, ask her friend…you know, the cop's daughter. Ask her about the man Sara left with. Stan Lupas. He has blond hair. She left with him to pick out headstones for her two recently departed brothers. That's my proof!"

Asher fell silent. If this was the truth, then he had to get to Sara. His eyes clouded as he looked at his father. He didn't know what to do. He was scared shitless, but he couldn't bear the thought of Sara being in Mr. D's clutches.

"What's the matter, punk? Are you going to cooperate with me or not?" he snarled. "You'd better make up your mind quick. I'm not a patient man."

He decided to play along for a few minutes just to buy some time. "I don't have a choice then," he said. He glanced at his father, motioning for him to get the officer.

"No games, Michaels. If the police find out where we're meeting, you'll never see your girlfriend alive again and I will come for you. You can't hide from me. You'll spend the rest of your short life looking over your shoulder. That's a promise!"

Asher nervously shifted his weight from one foot to the other. He needed to get as much information as he could just in case Mr. D really was telling the truth. Right now he didn't know what to believe. "I'll do what you say. You have my word," he said quietly.

The officer followed Bob Michaels into the living room and motioned to Asher.

"Where and what time?" Asher asked.

"Midnight. The old train depot," he ordered. "Don't bring anyone with you," he warned. "If I see any cops, Sara dies!"

"I won't." He paused. "Is she at the train depot now? Let me talk to her for a minute. Please!"

He laughed. "You really are stupid. Be at the depot at midnight. If you're even one minute late, she's dead." The line went silent.

Asher clicked off his phone. He shoved it in his pocket. His shoulders slumped as he looked at his father. "He wants me to meet him."

"What did he say about Sara Kane?" the officer asked.

"He said he has her." He shook his head. "But he has to be lying, right? She's at Taylor Trevors' house." His eyes searched the officer's for affirmation.

"We have a car watching the Trevors' house," the officer assured him. "Tell me everything he said."

Asher exhaled loudly. "He said he told Sara he was taking her to get headstones or something, and that Taylor Trevors will say the same thing." He chewed his bottom lip. "What if what he's saying is the truth? What if he somehow did get to Sara?" He swallowed hard.

****

Hunter sat across from Bella. "Sweetheart, what's troubling you? If it's anything to do with the wedding plans, we'll get it straightened out. It happens. I think you've been spending so much time planning our perfect wedding that you're wearing yourself out." He studied her closely. "Why don't you lie down for a while? You look exhausted."

"We need to talk, Hunter." She frowned. "I don't know what or who to believe any more." She met his eyes. "I'm filled with doubts, when this should be the happiest time of my life."

"Are you telling me that you're having second thoughts about marrying me?" he asked half-jokingly.

"I don't know," she admitted.

His eyebrows shot up. "You've got to be kidding me, Bella. What happened that could possibly change your mind? You mentioned you don't know who or what you can believe. If someone has said anything derogatory about me, I have the right to defend myself. It hurts me deeply that you would believe a rumor without discussing it with me."

She looked into his eyes and saw the pain in them. Was it real or was he faking? Why would Zoey lie? It had taken courage

193

for her to admit what she'd done. Bella had to give her credit for that, because as despicable as her admission was, Zoey had everything to lose and nothing to gain. And she was pregnant to boot.

"Bella? You've gone quiet. I want to know who's been spreading lies about me."

"I hope they are only lies, Hunter." No matter the outcome, she would still lose someone dear to her, or maybe both of them. If Zoey *was* lying for whatever reason, then their friendship would be over, but at least she would still have Hunter. If Zoey was telling the truth, then their friendship would still be over and she would lose Hunter, too. She looked into his eyes. "Zoey came over today." She watched his face closely, looking for a sign... any sign. The muscles in his jaw tightened. His eyes narrowed as he looked sharply at her.

"Why would Zoey, of all people, spread lies about me? It doesn't make sense. What did she say?" he demanded.

"My friendship with her is over," she said quietly.

"Good. I'm glad you didn't believe her vicious lies." He shook his head. "Why would she want to hurt you?" He smiled faintly. "Well, you certainly don't need friends like her."

She looked curiously at him. "I haven't even told you what she said, Hunter."

"It doesn't matter, does it? She's tried to destroy our happiness, and you put her in her place."

Bella closed her eyes for a second. She didn't want to lose him. She loved him so much that it hurt. Bella prayed he would voluntarily offer to take a paternity test to prove his fidelity to her. That would be the only way he could prove his innocence. She opened her eyes and looked hard at him. His right eye slightly twitched. "What Zoey said is very serious, Hunter."

194

He exhaled loudly. "What is it?" he asked tonelessly.

"I'll come right to the point." She took a deep breath, holding it in longer than necessary before letting it out. "Zoey said that you two had an affair."

"What?" His eyes grew wide with surprise, and then he laughed. "You've got to be kidding me. That's ridiculous."

"She told me it began shortly after you and I met, and it continued until recently," she continued.

"I'm glad you told her she was lying."

"Is she?" Bella asked, searching his eyes.

"Yes. She's a liar!" he said angrily. "She took every opportunity to throw herself at me. When I rejected her, she couldn't handle it and had to make up something that never existed."

"Why didn't you tell me? I certainly would have confronted her then."

"I didn't want you to be hurt, because I knew what her friendship meant to you. I told her how much I love you and nothing could come between us. She apologized and pleaded with me not to tell you."

She watched his face flush as he talked. She wondered if he was making excuses as he went. "Why would she tell me now then, Hunter? Especially if, as you say, she begged you not to tell me." She stared at him for a long minute. He avoided her eyes.

"I don't know, Bella. Maybe she's suffering from a mental disorder."

Bella stood up. "Zoey's not suffering from a mental illness, Hunter. If she's suffering from anything, it's guilt." She studied him, noticing how uncomfortable the conversation was making him. She wanted him to admit to the affair before she mentioned Zoey's pregnancy.

"What else did she say?" he asked, clenching his hands into

tight fists.

"You were only marrying me for the prestige my name would give you." She tried to stay in control, but her voice trembled. He was hiding the truth from her. She sensed it, and it was ripping her heart out. "Why, Hunter?"

"She's nuts! I thought we had something special together. Something no one could tear apart."

"Zoey was risking her future to tell me."

"What was she risking?" he smirked.

She stared at him in disbelief. "Her own relationship with Daniel."

His lips drew into a thin line. "She was probably just stringing him along until someone better came along."

"I don't believe that. She's not that type of person. When they got back together, it was the happiest I've ever seen her. She's never felt about any man the way she does about Daniel."

"No matter. Truthfully, I'm relieved that she won't be around to hurt you anymore. You don't need her." He reached for her. "All you need is me."

She pulled away from him. "Hunter, please tell me the truth...I'm begging you."

"I've told you the truth," he said. "But obviously you'd rather believe her over your fiancé." His shoulders slumped. "If you don't believe me, then what kind of future do we possibly have together?" His eyes softened. "We're the golden couple, honey. Can't you see that Zoey is jealous because of what you and I have together?"

"Why should she be jealous, Hunter? She's jeopardized her own future with Daniel. I don't see a motive here. She put her own reputation on the line."

He shook his head. "This is getting us nowhere. She's nothing but a vicious liar!" He glanced at his wristwatch. "I've got some work to do. We can finish this later. Maybe after you've had time to think about how your accusations are hurting me." He paused. "But I'll forgive you because I love you. That's just the type of man I am."

"I want to settle this now, Hunter. Zoey has never lied to me before," she said quietly.

He rubbed his jaw. "So I'm the liar. Is that what you believe, Bella?"

"Please just tell me the truth," she pleaded.

"I did. I told you that she tried to come on to me and I refused her advances."

"Hunter, Zoey told me that this is exactly what you would say."

He slowly let his breath out. "What do you want me to say, Bella? I love you and you are the woman I've chosen to spend the rest of my life with." His forehead wrinkled.

Bella cleared her throat. "Zoey's pregnant." She watched as the color drained from his face. "She says you're the father."

"What! Now I know she's gone completely mad."

"There's one way you can prove it, Hunter."

He lifted an eyebrow. "My word isn't enough?"

"The only way I'll have any peace of mind is if you submit to a paternity test. Until you do, we need to postpone the wedding." Hunter's forehead broke out with beads of perspiration. Bella had never seen him so uncomfortable. His usually cool demeanor was crumbling. She wanted him to tell her the truth no matter how much it would hurt her. "Will you get the test?"

"How far along is she?" he asked flatly.

"I don't know."

He sighed. "It could be months before the baby's born and

I'd be able to take the paternity test...not that the baby will be proven to be mine." He pursed his lips. "It's not fair to put our wedding off while we wait."

"Paternity tests can be given during the pregnancy," Bella told him. She saw his eyes cloud. She instinctively knew that he was looking for another excuse, but she wasn't going to give him the opportunity. "Hunter, will you take the test?"

"What happened was a stupid mistake. It didn't mean anything."

Bella's heart seized. "Zoey was telling the truth. Everything you've just said was a lie." Her eyes brimmed with tears.

He ran a hand over his chin. "Let me explain, honey," he said softly. "The night you and I met, Zoey had been giving me the come on all evening. I wasn't interested and ignored her. That must have upset her, because she began contacting me constantly and I told her I wanted her to stop. She did briefly, but then one night she called me and was very upset. I felt sorry for her. She asked if I would meet with her, just to talk. I went over to her apartment, and before the door had even closed behind us, she was all over me. I know it's no excuse, but I succumbed to her. I swear to you that it only happened that one time. Afterward I felt guilty and ashamed. I couldn't tell you, and I begged her not to. She's been holding it over my head ever since."

"Were you ever going to tell me?" Bella asked.

"Yes, I swear I was. I was going to after the wedding." He walked over to her and started to pull her close, but she froze when his fingertips touched her bare arms. "I'm not the one you should be angry with," he said. "Your best friend seduced me."

She was quiet for a few seconds. "I'm disgusted with the both of you. But mostly with you, Hunter. You violated something that I held precious. When you pledged your love to me and placed this ring on my finger," she slipped the ring from her finger and placed it in his hand, "I thought that you were pledging your fidelity to me."

"Bella, it was only one time. I swear. I made a mistake…I'm only human!" He tried to put the ring back on her finger.

She slapped his hand away. "No, Hunter. I think you're lying and that it happened more than one time. And I'll never be convinced that Zoey pushed herself at you. I think that you were the one who pursued her."

"No! It wasn't like that at all!"

"She's carrying your child."

"You don't know that." His eyes darkened. "I'll take the test." He paused. "Look, even if the baby's mine, I'll sue for custody and you and I can raise it."

Her eyes widened. "Are you out of your mind? Number one, I would never take Zoey's child from her, and number two, why would I want to raise a child with you that you conceived with another woman while you were engaged to me?" Anger started pushing past the hurt as she looked at him. She despised everything he stood for. "It's over. Get out of my house!"

"You don't mean that, Bella. We can work this out."

"I said get out before I have you thrown out!"

CHAPTER FOURTEEN

Zoey sat at her kitchen table sipping a cup of tea. Her head throbbed and the pain reliever she had taken twenty minutes earlier hadn't kicked in. She had never felt so low in her life. The two people she cared most about were now shattered because of her. She knew their lives would never be the same. She had violated everything dear to her, and knew she had no right to be forgiven. Even if they someday did choose to forgive her, the relationships could never be restored to what they once were. And she couldn't blame Bella or Daniel. They were both innocent victims who didn't deserve what she'd done to them.

She decided that she would pack up and leave the city. She didn't know where she would go or what would happen to her. All she knew was that she had to get away; away from the painful memories of her deceit and the love she had lost.

Her doorbell rang, but she did not attempt to answer. The caller persisted, so she finally got up and walked over to the door. She opened it a crack, but it was pushed with such a force that it sent her reeling backwards into the room.

"You couldn't keep your mouth shut, could you?" Hunter

yelled, grabbing her arm and pulling her to her feet.

She rubbed her arm. "I had to do the right thing. I couldn't live with myself anymore, Hunter. I love Daniel too much to have something like this deception hanging between us."

"Right! Pure and innocent Zoey decides to pull a morals act." He pulled her close. She could feel his hot breath on her face and it sickened her. "You couldn't have me, so you decided to fuck up my life!"

She grimaced. "You're wrong. I never loved you, Hunter."

"You're not going to get away with screwing up my life! No one double crosses me," he said.

"You screwed up your own life." She struggled to free herself from his hold, but his powerful arms kept a firm grasp on her. "Let go of me! You're hurting me!"

He laughed as he tightened his grip.

"You're hurting me, Hunter. Please let go," she pleaded, at the same time seeing the strange look in his eyes. The look terrified her. "Hunter, please let go. I'll tell Bella that I lied. Then you two can go ahead with your plans."

"No. It's too late for that," he snarled. "You told her you're pregnant."

"I've...I've already taken care of that decision," she stuttered.

"What do you mean?"

"I've decided to go away and raise the baby on my own."

He glared at her with a sickening grin.

****

Daniel walked into the house, surprised to find his partner waiting for him.

"Where the hell have you been?" Ben demanded, not giving him time for a greeting.

Daniel looked at him quizzically. "I went for a drive. I had some things on my mind and I needed to clear my head."

"You didn't answer your cell."

Daniel reached into his pocket. "Dammit. I must have accidentally hit the power button and turned it off."

"Taylor's been trying to reach you."

Daniel stiffened. "Is that why you're here? Has something happened to Taylor?"

"Taylor's fine, but this Mr. D has Sara Kane."

Daniel's mouth dropped open. "That's not possible. Sara went to pick out headstones for her brothers' graves. That's what Taylor told me."

"It was a setup, Daniel. The bastard pulled a fast one on us. There is no Drake Memorials or Stan Lupas in this entire city." He clenched his fists. "The Kanes never sent anyone here." He paused. "Asher Michaels is supposed to meet him tonight at the old train depot. If he doesn't show Mr. D has threatened to kill Sara."

Daniel anxiously looked around the room. "Where's Taylor?"

"Upstairs resting. Understandably, she's pretty shaken up. I thought she was going to have a breakdown or something, so your neighbor came over to take care of her."

"Good...good," he said, relieved that she was safe. "Do the Kanes know what's going on?"

"Not yet, but guess who has to tell them?"

Daniel shook his head. "I don't know how much more they can take. Let me check on Taylor for a minute."

"Okay, but don't be long. After we see the Kanes, we've got to plan our strategy with Michaels." He checked the time. "There's one more thing."

Daniel turned on the stairs and peered over the railing. "What?"

"Both of the Kane boys' motorcycles were pulled from the lake this morning."

"Shit!" He slammed his fist on the railing. "We've got to get that bastard!" he said as he headed up the stairs. He walked down the hall to Taylor's bedroom. He peeked into the darkened room and nodded to Mrs. Peters, a retired schoolteacher who lived next door. She sat by the bed patting Taylor's hand.

"Dad?" Taylor whispered.

He made his way over to her bed. "Honey, Sara's going to be just fine. We'll bring her home."

"Please, Dad."

"I promise." He kissed her cheek. He looked at the elderly woman. "Mrs. Peters, I hate to impose on you, but could you possibly stay with Taylor tonight?"

"Of course, Daniel," she answered.

****

Bill Kane led the detectives to the living room. Daniel noticed how spotless the room looked compared to his previous visits.

"Don't tell me anything if it's bad," Bill said in a shaky voice. "We can't take any more."

Mary Kane entered the room. Seeing the two detectives standing with her husband in the middle of her living room brought a look of horror to her face. "Bill!"

A shudder went through Daniel at the wounded sound that came from the grief stricken woman. Bill grabbed her hand and held on like he was holding on for his very life.

"This isn't easy," Daniel began.

"No!" Mary's hand flew to her mouth. "Not Sara! Is she—?"

"No, no," Daniel quickly assured her. "But we do have reason to believe that she may be in danger." He turned to Ben. "Detective Wilson will fill you in on the details." Daniel watched as Ben talked. He observed the parents, wondering what he would do if he were in their shoes. Ben's voice was low, deep, and filled with compassion as he gave them a detailed listing of the events that had transpired. When he told them about the motorcycles, the couple clung to one another as tears streamed down their faces.

"We've already lost our boys," Mary sobbed. "We can't lose Sara, too."

"We'll get him. We'll find Sara," Daniel promised.

Bill Kane swallowed rapidly. "After the funerals, we've arranged to go to rehab. We want to give Sara the parents she deserves." His voice broke. "But now we may never be given that chance."

****

Asher Michaels pleaded with his father. "Dad, I have to go. If I don't, I know he'll kill Sara."

Bob Michaels knew the risk involved. "Son, if you don't go and he comes after you as he said he would, the police have a better chance of catching him," he reasoned.

Asher's eyes filled with tears. "If I don't go he'll kill Sara. How could I ever live with myself, knowing I might have been able to save her? This is the best chance we have to get him now before he kills anyone else."

Daniel saw the torment in Bob Michaels' eyes. "He'll be covered. We've got the place staked out, and he may even be caught before Asher gets there."

"There isn't any other way?" the father asked apprehensively as he looked at Daniel.

"I'm afraid not," Daniel answered.

"If it's the only way," he said uneasily, looking at Asher.

****

Zoey struggled to pull the sheet around her naked body. She looked in horror as the white sheet quickly turned crimson. She tried to raise herself, but searing pain ripped through every nerve in her body. Zoey lay back, panting for a few minutes, and then attempted to lift her head, but a sickening dizziness overtook her.

God, help me! her mind screamed. She opened her mouth, but no words would come. Her mouth was filling with blood, which gurgled up from her throat. Zoey was growing weaker by the second, and every breath was becoming more difficult to take. She needed help...if she could only reach the phone. She willed herself to stretch her arm out and try to reach the phone on the bedside table. Zoey moved her arm slightly and a piercing sensation shot through her side. Her arm lay limp next to the gaping wound in her side. She felt the stickiness from the blood oozing out of it. Zoey was dying, and there was nothing she could do about it. The blood was thicker in her mouth now and it gurgled out, trickling over her lips.

Daniel, her mind cried. *I always loved only you.*

Her lips slightly parted and her eyes refused to focus anymore. A quiet peacefulness touched her soul when Daniel's image filled her mind. Then death slowly claimed her.

Chapter Fifteen

Mr. D waited impatiently for Asher Michaels to arrive. Tonight it would be over. Tomorrow he would make a fresh start, which included leaving the city for good. He smiled. Leaving would be the best thing he had ever done. That thought cheered him up. He deserved a fresh start, and that's what he would get. Mr. D would simply disappear. He had no friends here, so no one would notice he'd even gone. That suited him just fine.

"Where is that punk?" he muttered. He would give him ten more minutes, and if he didn't show, Sara Kane was done. He hoped Michaels would ride in like Sara Kane's knight in shining armor. Michaels didn't look like he could fight his way out of a paper bag. Mr. D would show the little bastard what a real man was made of. He laughed.

His eyes shifted and focused on a faint beam of light making its way up the path. He stayed hidden in the shadows and watched as Asher stopped his motorcycle.

Asher got off his bike and trembled slightly as he glanced around the deserted train station.

Mr. D slowly came out of the shadows. "Right on time," he

said. "I'll take you to her."

****

Asher was momentarily startled. "Which one is she in?" He peered uneasily at the eerie surroundings as shadows from abandoned buildings loomed like menacing fingers ready to snatch him from the spot on which he stood. He hoped the police were watching him. He doubted Sara was in any of those buildings, because if she was, she would have been rescued by now. Mr. D was too slick. He wished the cops would take him right now, but if they did, he might not tell where he'd hidden Sara.

"Come on. We need to take my car."

"What about my bike?"

"Leave it."

"Where is your car?" Asher asked as his knees weakened.

"Follow me."

Asher followed him up a winding, narrow path. The flashlight the man held cast a steady beam of light through the tangled undergrowth. Asher tried to focus on the thin line of light, but his eyes drifted to the darkness on either side of him. He stumbled, and then fell to his knees.

Mr. D stopped, annoyed. "Get up! I don't have all night!"

Asher pulled himself to his feet. He rubbed his knee and felt a small bump forming. "How much farther is it?"

"Right ahead," he answered.

Asher looked at the unfamiliar road. Only someone who knew the area well would ever know this road existed. The cops better be tailing him.

"Here we are," the man announced, walking to a large clump of bushes.

****

Daniel stood behind a tree peering out into the darkness. "We'd better get up there," he whispered to Ben. "If we don't, we'll lose him. And I don't even want to think what he'll do to those kids."

"Me either," Ben agreed. "I was positive we'd find Sara in one of the buildings. I don't know where the hell he could have taken her." He signaled to the backup officers.

****

Bella walked through the rooms of her apartment looking at all the exquisite possessions her family had accumulated throughout their lives. She was a wealthy woman, but her money meant nothing to her now. She was lonely. For the first time in her life, she realized that she didn't have anyone to share her life with. She had more than her share of acquaintances, but no deep, true lasting friendships. Money had always been the issue. Whenever she thought someone truly wanted to be her friend, the matter of money seemed to come up. Funding was needed for this project or that charity. Soon, she realized that no one cared for her as much as they did for her money.

Zoey had been the only true friend she'd had. But why had Zoey betrayed her? What had she done to deserve this? And Hunter; how could he have hurt her so deeply? Why? Now he was lost to her, too. How she longed for his strong, safe arms. Being wrapped in his embrace had always made her feel so safe and secure. Now there was no one left. There was nothing to look forward to. Each day would be the same, dragging endlessly on.

Bella lay down on her sofa hoping for some sleep, but knowing that sleep would elude her. Her tortured mind would keep taking her back over the events of the day. She couldn't stand the desperate loneliness overtaking her. She didn't care anymore. Bella would rather have Hunter and Zoey still with her than to be totally alone. She would find a way to work through the pain of what they had done, but right now, she could no longer stand the emptiness engulfing her.

She picked up the phone and called Zoey's number and let it ring several times before giving up. Next, she tried Hunter's number. Her call went to voice mail. She didn't leave a message. Bella set her cell phone down. Now she felt worse than she had before. She was crushed. She didn't know what to do, but she knew that she couldn't just sit here and do nothing. If she did, she would surely lose her mind.

****

Asher was shaking when he got into the car, and Mr. D's sharp eyes on him unnerved him. He was scared. He would never have agreed to this if it weren't for Sara. Sara was all that mattered right now. He had to keep his cool and concentrate on her.

Mr. D started the car. He glanced at Asher. "Feels like you're taking the last trip of your life, huh?"

Asher nervously cleared his throat. "I don't know why you're doing this. Sara and I don't even know your real name."

"By tomorrow at this time I'll be long gone, and no one will ever know who I am," he sneered.

"Please don't hurt Sara," he pleaded.

"It's too late for that now. I told you, no one, no matter who, double crosses me, punk!" He tilted his head. "Now you're going to suffer the consequences."

"But I didn't!" he insisted. "Sara never did anything to you either."

He tightly gripped the steering wheel. "We've already had this discussion."

"But—"

"Shut up!"

Asher sat back in the seat. As worried as he was right at this moment, he wondered what Sara was going through. She had to be terrified out here all alone, not knowing what Mr. D's next move would be. He wondered if the police were really following his every move. He had no way of knowing. Mr. D had eluded them before. How could he be sure the man hadn't given them a cold trail again? But Asher suddenly realized that if Sara and he were to be killed, at least she wouldn't be alone. Then the thought struck him that Sara might already be dead.

****

Bella pounded on Zoey's apartment door, but no one answered. "Where are you?" she whispered aloud. She reached into her purse for the key Zoey had given her when she'd moved into the apartment. Bella had never used it, but Zoey had insisted she take it as a precaution should anything happen. She unlocked the door, opened it, and then stepped inside, closing the door behind her.

"Zoey," she called as she entered the living room and turned on a lamp. Zoey obviously isn't home, she thought. She'd wait here until Zoey returned. Something caught her eye. Zoey's purse was on the sofa. Zoey wouldn't have gone out without her purse. Maybe she was taking a shower or had gone to bed. But wouldn't she have heard her calling out to her? An uneasy feeling crept over her. Bella slowly crept through the dark apartment, turning on lights as she walked. She peered into the bathroom. The last room was the bedroom. She opened the door to the darkened room. "Zoey," she called softly. "Are you here?" Bella made her way over to the bed and turned on the small lamp on the bedside table. The soft glow illuminated the room. She looked at the bed. Zoey's open, lifeless eyes greeted her. Bella let out a blood curdling scream.

****

"Where is Mr. D going?" Ben asked.

"Wish I knew," Daniel sighed.

"We'll get him this time," Ben assured him.

"I don't want either of those kids hurt." Daniel stared at the road ahead.

"They won't be," Ben insisted. "It'll be over soon."

"Yeah, you're right. How's Josh doing? You going to be able to have him for part of the summer?" Daniel asked.

Ben grimaced. "Yeah, I think so, but only if I meet Clare's demands."

Daniel laughed. "Clare's demands? What the hell are you talking about?"

Ben sniffed. "Just what I said. I can see my son if I raise the child support and alimony payments again. She's up and down."

"You've got to be kidding!"

"No, deadly serious. Seems the boyfriend—creative genius that he is—needs to work on a project, which means that he will have no income and Clare wants to help him out."

"Ben, you need a good lawyer."

He slowly let his breath out. "Yeah, but I can't afford a good one. And what's the use? She'll bleed me dry as usual, with or without one."

"How are you going to afford to pay her more?"

He shrugged. "I don't know. I'll think of something. All I care about is my son. I'd give my life for him."

"I know you would," Daniel replied. "You know if there's anything I can do, just ask."

"Thanks, I'll keep that in mind." He stared straight ahead.

****

Mr. D stopped the car, and then turned to Asher. "I'm only going to tell you this once. Any funny stuff and you won't get a chance to see your girlfriend. I see any cops and no one will ever find her, and you and the cops will be dead." He opened the car door. "Do I make myself clear?"

"Yes," Asher said in a shaky voice.

"Okay, let's go."

Asher was perspiring so badly that his sweaty hand could barely grasp the door handle.

"Come on," the man said impatiently.

"I'm coming." He heard the latch click. He pushed the door open, feeling the rush of cool air on his face. It seemed to revive him a little.

Mr. D led the way to a building Asher never knew existed, tucked into a densely wooded area. If the cops weren't following them, they may never find Sara or him. Mr. D threw the door open, then shined a flashlight around the room. Asher's eyes followed the beam of light until it rested on a form huddled in a corner of the dusty dank room. He ran to Sara and gathered her into his arms.

"Asher?" she whimpered.

"I'm here, Sara. You didn't think I'd let anything happen to you, did you?" He tried to keep his voice light.

She rested her head on his shoulder. "He tricked me. He's going to kill us, Asher!"

"No," he whispered. "The cops followed me here, but he doesn't know it." He ran his hand over her smooth cheek. "We're going to be fine. Don't worry. Just take my lead on whatever I say. Okay?"

"Okay." She squirmed uncomfortably. "Would you see if you can get him to untie me?"

"Can I untie her?" Asher called loudly to the man who was standing near the door, peering into the darkness.

He looked at Asher. "If you don't try anything stupid."

"I won't," Asher answered. He removed the ropes from Sara as quickly as he could. She stood unsteadily, stretching her cramped legs. "Have you had anything to eat or drink?" he asked.

"No."

"Do you have any food or water?" Asher yelled again to Mr. D.

"What the hell do you think this is, a hotel?" the man asked in a surly tone. He shoved his hands into his pockets. "Just get your goodbyes over with, and be grateful I'm giving you that consideration! Hurry up...I don't have all night!" he ordered.

Asher held Sara tightly. "I promise you that I won't let him hurt you. When we get out of here I'll buy you the biggest pizza you've ever had."

"Will we get out of here, Asher?" she whimpered.

He took a deep breath. "We will, Sara."

****

"Hurry it up, you two." Mr. D's fingers clamped around the handle of his knife. He loved the rush of adrenaline as he anticipated plunging the knife into the girl's ripe, young flesh. A rustling outside the shack caught his attention. He listened for a few seconds and decided it must have been an animal scampering through the woods.

He walked over to where Sara and Asher stood. "I want you to stand over here," he said to Asher as he motioned him to his left side.

"Can I have a few more minutes alone with her?"

"No. You've had enough time." He walked toward Sara, stopped in front of her, and then stood staring at her for a few

213

seconds. "You're a real beauty," he finally said, running his hand down her arm.

Sara pushed him away. "Don't!"

He liked the feel of her smooth, cool flesh. "Why not, baby? I'll bet you wouldn't complain if your boyfriend here did that to you. Am I right?" He kissed her cheek. He loved seeing the fear in her eyes.

"Get away from her!" Asher yelled.

Mr. D laughed. "Getting jealous, punk?"

Asher looked around for something, anything he could use as a weapon, but saw nothing. Where the hell are the cops? he wondered. They should have barged in here by now. He could escape, but then he would be signing Sara's death certificate for her. Mr. D would surely kill her and then come after him. "Please don't hurt her!"

He turned and shined the light in Asher's face. "What are you going to do about it?"

Asher held his arm up to shield his face from the blaring light, and then ran and lunged at Mr. D. He caught Asher by the arm, and with one swift movement flung him, causing Asher to fall to the floor.

Sara screamed.

He stood in front of her. "Shut up!"

Sara began to sob. "Please don't hurt us." He grabbed her arm and held the knife to her throat. "Please don't," she pleaded. "I'll do whatever you say. Just don't hurt Asher and me." He grinned. "Not so tough now, are you, Michaels?" he asked with his back to the teen.

"Leave her alone!" Asher screamed as he suddenly charged Mr. D from behind, pummeling the man with his closed fists. Mr. D released Sara, turned, raised his fist, and struck Asher with such a forceful blow to the side of his head that Asher reeled backwards, but managed to stay on his feet.

Sara screamed.

The scream sent shivers up Mr. D's spine. He loved that sound. It never failed to unleash a power in him that he couldn't explain. He would have slashed the boy, but he wanted Asher to watch while he carved up Sara before finishing him off.

****

At that moment, Ben burst through the door, with Daniel at his heels. "Throw your weapon down!" he demanded as he aimed his gun at Mr. D. "Hands up!"

Sara ran to where Asher stood.

"Asher, get Sara out of here! Now!" Daniel ordered. "Hurry!"

Asher grabbed Sara's hand and they tore out of the shack.

"Throw the knife down, now!" Ben ordered.

Mr. D. grinned as he took a few steps toward Ben. He lowered the knife to his side. "What are you going to do now, Ben?" He laughed. "What do you think is going to happen to you?" Daniel flashed a light in the man's face as he kept his gun aimed at him. The man smiled as he ripped off his mustache and wig. "Surprise!" he said, tossing the glasses to the ground.

Daniel was stunned as he studied the familiar face. "You!" he shouted, as he kept the light aimed on the man's face.

"You know this guy?" Ben asked. "You know *Mr. D*?"

"Yeah, I know him all right. His name is Hunter Tucker."

Hunter grinned. "Benny boy, don't act like we're strangers."

"I don't believe it," Ben stuttered. "You killed all those people."

Daniel looked at Ben and noticed how pale he'd become. "What's going on, Ben?"

"He didn't tell you about our business relationship?" Tucker asked. "Just when you think you know someone," he said mockingly.

"Shut up, Tucker!" Ben ordered.

"What business relationship?" Daniel asked.

"Hey, Ben, did Daniel tell you how good Zoey is in the sack? I did her real good tonight," he said. "And then I got rid of her and that fucking bastard she was carrying."

Daniel's face twitched. "You sonofabitch!" he raged as he aimed his gun at him.

"Ben, call him off or you'll go down with me!" Hunter ordered.

"Daniel, keep your cool! He's lying. Cuff him."

"Oh, Benny boy, I'm not lying. I've got proof. I've got tapes of every one of our transactions. Tapes, Benny. You didn't think I'd be stupid enough to cut you in and not have some security, did you? If I go down, I drag you with me."

"Ben, what's he talking about?" Daniel asked.

"He was blackmailing me for part of the take. Tell him, Ben! Tell him!" Hunter shouted.

Daniel shook his head. "No, Ben, not you. Tell me it isn't true."

Ben kept silent.

"God! Why, Ben?"

Ben shook his head. "I couldn't keep up...the divorce cost me everything. But Clare always wanted more. You know that. More than I could give her. I don't know. The money was good. More than I'd ever make—"

"Dammit, Ben! You're a good cop! All those murders—"

"I knew nothing about the murders," Ben broke in. "I knew about the drugs. That's all I knew. I swear to you, Daniel. I would never kill anyone!"

"Poor Danny," Hunter taunted. "What a night…you've lost your girlfriend and your partner."

Daniel grabbed Ben's arm. "Give me the gun, Ben. I have to take you in."

"I can't do that, Daniel."

"Ben, I can't let you go. Toss your gun."

"No."

"It's over, Ben. The place is surrounded by now. You don't stand a chance," Daniel said.

"Call them in, Daniel," Ben said quietly.

Daniel grabbed his police radio and clicked it repeatedly, but it was silent.

"A glitch." Ben's voice was quiet.

"What?" Daniel's eyes slanted. "They're right outside this door! You set this up yourself."

"Daniel, if they were, don't you think they would have come busting in by now?" He eyed him evenly.

"Damn you, Ben!" He pointed to his partner. "You sonofabitch! You set me up! You planned this with him. That's why he knew the exact time to come to my house to get Sara. That's why he knew our every move!" He swallowed hard.

"Shut up," Ben ordered. "I told you I didn't know about the murders or Sara's abduction."

"You're just as guilty as he is!" Daniel raged.

"I said shut up!" Ben said, suddenly grabbing Daniel's arm and twisting it until Daniel's gun fell to the floor. "Do him," Ben said. "Come on, Tucker!"

"Ben, think about what you're doing. You'll never get away with it," Daniel said.

"Do it!" Ben ordered Hunter. "Now."

"Wait!" Daniel reasoned. "Think about your son, Ben. You'll

never see Josh again."

"Leave my son out of it," Ben said calmly. "He'll never know."

"You don't think you'll get away with this, do you? Maybe we can work something out if you really did have no knowledge of the murders."

"Like Zoey and I worked it out," Hunter taunted. "Hey, Danny, did she come for you like she did for me? All those nights you thought she was home pining for you, she was under me begging for more. She couldn't get enough of me." He licked his lips, making smacking sounds.

"You bastard!" Daniel pulled free from Ben and lunged at Tucker. He grabbed Hunter's wrist, trying to wrestle the knife from his tight grip. His hand slipped and the sharp blade of the knife cut into his palm.

"She was so good," Hunter taunted.

"You bastard!" Daniel shouted. Before he could utter another word, Hunter plunged the knife into his chest. Daniel's body was propelled backwards. Tucker immediately pulled the knife out of him. Daniel stared in horror at the bloody knife, then at Ben. The realization of his mortal life leaving him engulfed him as the burning pain washed over his body.

"Give me the car keys. You did get me the car, didn't you?" Hunter demanded. He walked towards Ben. "Answer me, Wilson." He pointed the bloody knife in front of Ben.

Ben aimed his gun at him.

Tucker smirked. "You're going to shoot me?" He moved closer.

Ben pulled the trigger. Hunter hit the floor with a loud thud. He heard Daniel moaning and walked to where he lay, then squatted and flashed the light on him as he examined the wound.

Blood was soaking the floor where Daniel lay. Ben removed his jacket and placed it over the wound. He picked up his transmitter. "Wilson here. Officer down." He gave the location.

"Ben," Daniel whispered. "Ben."

"I'm here."

"Ben, do something for me."

"What, Daniel?"

"Tell Taylor I love her." He could barely get the words out. "Zoey loved me, Ben."

Ben patted Daniel's shoulder. "I'm sorry it had to end this way."

Daniel's mind drifted. The pain slowly left his body and was replaced with peace. He was in a beautiful green meadow. It was a beautiful day, sunny and bright. Zoey sat on a blanket while he rested his head in her lap as she gently ran her fingers through his hair. He looked across the meadow and watched Taylor pick a bouquet of flowers. Her golden hair glistened in the warm afternoon sun. She began walking toward them and then stopped. She held out her hand to him. He tried to sit up, but couldn't. He stretched his arms in her direction. "Taylor, wait!" he called.

"What did you say, Daniel?" Ben asked.

Daniel's body twitched as he struggled to get up. He watched as Taylor turned and began to walk in the opposite direction. He looked up into Zoey's loving eyes. She smiled at him. It was the most beautiful smile he had ever seen. Taylor would come back. He and Zoey would wait together for her return. Zoey leaned down and kissed him. It was the sweetest kiss he had ever tasted. He smiled as he closed his eyes.

****

"Daniel," Ben said as he looked into Daniel's vacant eyes. He felt for a pulse, but found none.

Seconds later the room was swarming with police. "Sorry. Something went wrong with the transmitter," an officer said. "We lost you guys about thirty minutes ago."

Ben wiped the tears from his face as he looked into the officer's eyes.

"Is he...?" the officer asked without finishing the sentence.

Ben nodded.

CHAPTER SIXTEEN

Bella parked in front of the Davis Dance Studio. She turned off the ignition and sat staring at the vacant building. She couldn't accept the fact that Zoey was really dead. She thought about all the times she had dropped into the studio, catching Zoey in the middle of a class. For a second she almost believed that if she got out of the car and walked through the door, Zoey would be there to greet her. Then she would know that all of this was only a bad dream. But the headlines from the newspaper on the seat next to her screamed out the truth. Nothing would ever be the same. Hunter had destroyed so many lives. She stared at the newspaper. Zoey smiled at her from the picture. Bella was still in shock after learning the truth about Hunter. It chilled her to realize that she had almost married this monster.

She started the car. Bella had closed up her apartment, and was finally going to stand on her own two feet and take control of her life. Instead of sitting in the background, she had decided to take an active position in the company her father had left her so many years before. She looked at the studio once more. "Goodbye, my friend," she whispered as she drove off.

****

Ben Wilson took Daniel's belongings from his desk and stuffed the items into a cardboard box. He picked up a picture and looked at it for a long minute. In the picture, Daniel had his arm protectively around Taylor as she sat on her first bicycle.

His thoughts turned to Taylor. She was without a mother and father now, but she was strong and he knew she would go on with her life. He wasn't going to feel guilty for the deaths. Hunter Tucker did those all on his own. He was sorry, though, that Daniel had to find out about the money. If Hunter had only kept his mouth shut, then Daniel might still be alive. But Ben had had no choice. Daniel would never have let him get away with what he had done. Some other cop might have, but not Daniel Trevors. His integrity wouldn't allow it. Ben's secret would be safe now. He shook his head as he picked up the remaining items, set them in the box, and then closed it.

****

Sara held tight to Taylor's hand. "I'm going to miss you, Taylor."

Taylor smiled at her. "We'll text every day."

Sara frowned. "People always say that, but they never do."

"Well, we will," Taylor assured her. "Remember, always friends. We'll always be there for each other no matter what."

"I wish we could go back in time."

"Me, too, but we can't. We have to go forward."

"Asher feels responsible for your father's death."

Taylor frowned. "He shouldn't. If it wasn't for him, Tucker would have killed you."

"How can you be so brave, Taylor?"

"I don't know. I have so many good memories of my dad that I try to only think of that." She took a last look around her bedroom. "It's going to feel strange living with my aunt. I only met her once when I was four."

"She seems nice," Sara said.

"Yeah, she is. She's helped me a lot." She picked up her suitcase.

They walked downstairs and into the entrance hall. Taylor stopped briefly and took one final look around.

"Are you okay?" Sara asked. She slipped her arm through Taylor's.

"Yeah, I'm a Trevors, remember?" She opened the door, and then quickly shut it.

"What's the matter?"

"I almost forgot. Some thumb drives came in the mail for my dad. There was a note, and it said if my dad wasn't available, to make sure that they were given to the police commissioner. My aunt's going to stop at the police station on our way to the airport."

"Why not give them to Detective Wilson and let him give them to the commissioner?"

Taylor shook her head. "We would have, but he's taken a leave of absence and is out of state for a few weeks. So we decided that we better give the tapes to the police commissioner in case they're for an important case Dad was working on."

Sara sighed deeply. "I'll be staying with Asher and his family until my parents get out of rehab."

"I think it's great about your parents, and about Asher's mother coming back."

"She's nice, and Asher is so different now."

"I guess this is what they mean when they tell you that something good can come out of even the worst situations."

Sara nodded in agreement. "Yeah, but it's still going to be

hard on all of us."

"Just remember, I'm only a phone call away. And Aunt Dee said you can come stay any time you want to."

Sara smiled. "I intend to."

Taylor opened the door and she and Sara walked outside. She set the suitcase down, and then closed the door for the last time.

Susan K. Droney

AUTHOR

Writing is Susan's number one passion. When she isn't writing, she enjoys reading, spending time in her garden, and visiting family and friends. She has many novels, short stories, and magazine articles to her credit. Raised in western New York, she now resides in New Jersey. For information about Susan's current and upcoming titles, please visit http://www.susandroney.com or http://susandroney.blogspot.com